Voodoo

Mystery

Tour

Thank you for your laughter + support !

Monique Jacob

Monique Jacob

US Soft Cover Edition

Published by Lulu.com, USA

Produced by Filidh Publishing

Victoria, British Columbia, Canada

ISBN 978-1-304-42997-1

Copyright: September 2013, Monique LeBlanc

(aka Monique Jacob)

All rights reserved.

filidhbooks.com

Cover Art by Kimberley Zutz.

Other books by Monique Jacob:

Tye Dye Voodoo, 2012

Acknowledgements:

You need far more than just a storyteller to create a good book. Thanks to Kimberley Zutz for another great cover; Jennifer Peddle for her recipes; Diane Cliffe for wrangling my mushy prose into shape; Zoe Duff and Filidh Publishing for making it all possible.

one more for chilly bear

ONE

Morning mist curled over the glassy surface of Cricket Lake, softening the spiky tree-line on the far shore.

Phineas Marshal sat in a purple leather chair on the porch that spanned the width of his house. He'd designed it to face the water so he could keep an eye on the lake while he drank his morning coffee.

Phin was on his third cup and he could feel the caffeine starting the jitter in his hands that came with anything more than the two cups he usually had before breakfast.

But he'd wanted that extra jolt to keep him alert. He'd woken from the dream where he'd dived into the centre of the lake, following a brilliant light. He'd felt the familiar terror of running out of air as he swam deeper and the light engulfed him. A brief pang of loss on waking had him worried about some sick part of him that welcomed the nightmare.

He'd tripped and nearly fallen twice while stumbling from his bed to the front door, and had stood on the cold porch boards for long minutes, convincing himself the eerie glow on the lake came from the nearly-full moon, and not from its watery depths.

He'd then repeated out loud the four words which had become a soothing mantra over the past two years: "I drowned the bogeyman." It hadn't seemed as funny as it usually did, but nothing much was funny in the creepy hours before dawn.

Phin sipped his coffee and grimaced. It had cooled. He downed the rest in one gulp and got up to start another pot. Before stepping through the door and into his kitchen he glanced over his shoulder for one more look at the calm water. Tendrils of mist faded in the first rays of the sun. In the cool morning light he could almost believe it was as harmless as any other lake.

He'd been watching it for nearly two years and had seen no sign of trouble. But he wasn't fooled. If his dreams were any indication, the lake was as strong as ever but he seemed safe from its lure while he was awake.

Those dreams – which were as regularly-scheduled as a television series – had initially been so compelling that sometimes he'd only awakened as his feet hit the cold water. He'd overcome those early sleep-walking episodes by leaving obstacles in the path from his bed to the door. His subconscious had quickly learned to wake him up while still in bed rather than in a heap of furniture, covered in bruises.

Phin turned on the kitchen light, squinting in the harsh glow of the overhead fluorescents. The kitchen was utilitarian and spartan. Manly steel appliances along one wall, a simple wooden table with two chairs, and the minimum number of dishes he had been able to get away with.

The fresh coffee had just finished its last drip when he heard a quiet knock at the door. He considered not answering but his light was on – a clear sign that he was up. He glowered at the door then smelled the distinctive odour of pipe smoke wafting through the open window.

Toby Greer. The old man had moved into the farthest of the three cabins next to Phin's house and had mostly kept to himself. He'd paid for the entire summer and was writing his memoirs. Phin had worked hard to not roll his eyes when he'd heard that, having visions of ridiculous romantic prose and scenes of exaggerated exploits.

But he'd revised his first impression when Mabel, cornering the man at the grocery store, found out he was a retired journalist. She'd then called her librarian friend and discovered that he'd worked most of his career as a war correspondent. On his last assignment, caught between two factions of a violent civil war in Central America, Toby Greer had spent four years locked in a cell the size of a closet.

Phin liked the old guy, and was glad he'd put on fresh coffee. "Hope you like your coffee black," he said as he opened the door. "The cream is at the chunky stage that doesn't look pretty in something you want to drink."

"Black is fine. Cream doesn't do my innards any favours."

Phin snickered. "Innards. You sound like Mabel."

"If you're referring to the diminutive woman's charm and humour, then I accept the compliment."

"Even funnier, considering you're not at all her type."

"I haven't been anyone's type for most of my life," Toby said solemnly.

They carried mugs of steaming coffee out to the porch and sat watching the first swallows of the day hunting along the shore.

"I do like your choice of patio furniture," Toby said as he settled into a purple leather chair. "Are they from an RV?"

"Vintage 1997 Ford Econoline Custom Van," Phin answered and thumped the padded arm of his seat. "Got them at the Ruby Creek swap meet. Apparently they outlasted the van that rusted out from under them."

Phin had lashed eight milk crates together, on their sides with the openings facing out. He'd then bolted the two seats from the van onto a sheet of plywood, which he attached to the crate platform. Mabel had tacked a strip of fabric along the edge of the wood, creating a curtain that hid the plastic crates and their jumbled contents.

"Is it true you were a prisoner of war?"

"Is it true you're a voodoo witch doctor?"

Phin scowled and gulped his coffee, which was scorching hot. He spluttered and spat most of it onto his feet, much to the old man's amusement.

"It would seem we both have touchy issues."

Toby reached into his pocket and drew out a wrinkled pouch of fragrant leaves. He filled his pipe and tamped the tobacco down with a yellowed thumb.

Phin wished, for the tiniest moment, he'd never quit smoking when he was a younger man. There was something about the ritual of preparing to smoke that soothed the nerves and allowed a mind time to calmly consider words before speaking them aloud. "How do you like your cabin?"

"Oh, it'll do," Toby said distractedly. He struck a wooden match and held the flame to the bowl of his pipe, drawing steadily until the packed tobacco glowed and crackled.

"A lot of people put a lot of work into building these cabins," Phin said with what he hoped was nonchalance.

"It's a cabin," Toby countered. "I've rented dozens of them, and they've all been more or less the same." The corner of his mouth twitched. "Four walls. Smell of cedar – usually by a lake, or at least near enough to matter. No different than any other cabin I've ever seen."

He blew several smoke rings and watched them drift toward the water. "From what I've heard, you slapped them together in record time for tourist season."

"Mabel had this list of people who were waiting to rent by the week," Phin grumbled. He thumped his mug down on the porch railing and went inside for the coffee pot, snagging a cardboard baker's box from the counter on his way back.

"How do your innards like muffins?" He held out the box to Toby, who grinned and helped himself to two.

TWO

A harsh buzz pierced the quiet and pulled Dee Berkeley out of her reverie. She yawned and shook her head to clear it, wishing she'd had more than three hours' sleep before heading out to start the day's bread. She glanced up again at the lightening sky, with its trails of sunrise-painted clouds drifting past. It was going to be a gorgeous day, which meant a very busy day for the café.

She sighed and stood up from her seat by the window. She was already behind schedule and she had a lot to do before leaving. She wished she didn't have to drive to the city today.

Dee pulled open the door to her main bread oven, squinting against the blast of heat. The door moved smoothly on its hinges, and stayed exactly where she left it. She had finally stopped worrying about the door slowly closing on her while she was removing trays of bread, like the doors of the old ovens had sometimes done.

She removed six trays that each held six loaf pans and set them on the side counters to cool. As usual, the loaves were perfect golden brown mounds. Dee reset the oven's temperature and closed the door. She turned to the double-door freezer for cookie batter and nearly ran into a tiny woman with thick glasses and frizzy white hair.

"Mabel!" she squeaked in fright. "You shouldn't sneak up on me like that. I could have been carrying a hot tray from the oven."

"Yum. I could think of worse ways to get a free breakfast." Mabel reached up and wiped a smudge of flour off Dee's cheek. "I swear you're skinnier than the last time I saw you, Chickadee."

"Oh come on, Mabel," Dee said, smiling at her aunt. "You saw me just last night."

"I can't decide if I should be worried about you or if I should just keep throwing compliments your way."

"I feel fantastic, so I'll take the compliments, thank you very much." Dee filled a kettle and set it on the stove to boil.

"Earl Grey ok for you?" She turned around in time to catch Mabel breaking off a chunk of steaming bread right out of a pan. "You should have said you were hungry. I've got some yoghurt and granola."

"Are you kidding? When there's this little bite of heaven?" She stuffed the warm bread in her mouth and rolled her eyes as she chewed. She chose two cups from a shelf and put them next to the teapot Dee had set on the little table.

"Do you still have any of my jam left?" Mabel asked, while she helped herself to another hunk of bread.

"I thought you finished the last jar on the weekend." Dee poured them each a fragrant cup of tea. She had thought the drawing on the jam jars' labels was a joke on Mabel's part: a strawberry superimposed on a large garlic bulb. There hadn't been much garlic in the jam, just enough to ruin the sweet berries for Dee.

"It took me two years to go through that batch. Maybe I'll cut the recipe in half this time."

"Why not try something with ginger this time?" Dee loved her aunt, but that jam-making spree had left a garlic miasma that had taken days to dissipate.

Mabel pulled one of Dee's cookbooks off the shelf. It was easy to tell which books were Dee's favourites. They were stained and battered, with pages torn out and taped to the walls, scribbled with her notes and recipe adjustments. But most were brand new and had never been opened. When the old bakery had burned to the ground Dee had lost years' worth of recipes, many of her own creation. She'd tried to make up for the loss by purchasing every new book on baking she found online.

"I really need to find something new and different for next year's cooking contest," Mabel said. "I hope they come up with the theme sooner this time. I could have used more than a week to work on my pies." Mabel slapped the book shut and clamped it under one arm. "I'm gonna borrow this for a couple of days, if that's ok with you."

"Sure," Dee said with a grin. "Just put it with all the others you've 'borrowed'. I'll come up and get it if I need it."

"I've got to go let Peg out. She climbs these stairs amazingly well for a three legged cat, but can't quite get the hang of going down. She's fallen down twice now, and won't even try anymore. Can't blame her, poor old thing."

"Just be back by eleven, please. Penny won't be in until noon and I have to get home to feed Mom before we go, otherwise she'll try to use the stove again."

"No worries, Dee. I'll be back in a flash. I have to inventory all the stuff out front. It looks like it's gonna be a sunny weekend and I want to be sure to have lots of goodies for the tourists to buy. I'll be too busy once our retreat group arrives."

"Are you sure it's a good idea to have a group rental so soon? Phin's just barely got those cabins finished. He has plenty of detail work that won't ever get done if they're always full."

"The group from our last séance had so much fun they went off and told everyone we were going to offer full weekend retreats. I had the cabins booked up within a couple of days. I can't wait to tell Phineas." She winked at her niece. "How do you think he'll like having our next séance on the beach across the road from the cabins?"

"Don't go making any crazy plans. You know how uncomfortable he gets when you change things on him."

"Yeah, but that's when he's at his most brilliant," Mabel said with a grin. "When he has no idea what comes next, he stops relying on what he thinks should happen. That's when the magic flies."

THREE

Phin assessed the whine of the bicycle's tires on the asphalt as he pedaled faster. The newly-oiled chain wasn't giving him the extra speed he'd hoped to get but he did like the wider tires he'd traded for. With a large basket on the front and a cart towed behind – both usually full – he'd needed to beef up his bicycle.

His keen hearing picked out a tinny metallic shriek from one of the fittings he'd welded onto the bike's frame. He swerved left and right a few times to test it.

Left, definitely left. He'd have to check his weld, though maybe it was just the weight he was carrying that was overbalancing things a bit. There wasn't much left of the original bicycle Phin had found rusting in the basement of the house he'd inherited. He'd strengthened and expanded the frame, and replaced the narrow seat with a wider one taken off a tractor. Phin had bartered for most of what he'd needed to rebuild the bicycle at the monthly swap meet. The only parts he'd bought new were the brakes.

Phin checked over his shoulder as he changed lanes, and nearly jabbed his eye on the end of the wooden staff that was clamped to the bicycle's frame. He cursed and made a mental note to reset the clamps a little farther back. It wouldn't do to poke himself in the eye every time he had to transport a walking stick to the café.

He was pleased with the way the staff had turned out, and knew that Mabel would love it. He'd stained it a rich mahogany, which had settled deeply into the wavy designs he'd carved into the oak. Then he'd sanded the dark stain off the raised designs and re-stained the whole staff red. The darker etchings stood out against the red, and from a distance it was hard to tell if the designs were raised or cut deeply.

He'd added his signature bones and pebbles, gluing them onto the top eight inches of the staff to create a textured grip. He loved the way the smooth stones and bones felt in his hand. Before gluing them on, he'd soaked the bones overnight in a diluted stain and again for a short time in a bucket of bleach, which had left the bones looking as if they'd accumulated years of dirt – or blood – in their creases. It gave the staff a darker, graver look than any other he'd carved so far.

He rounded the corner onto Main Street and nearly ran over Tammy and her horde of tiny fluffy dogs. He slammed to a stop. Tammy shrieked and the dogs attacked the bicycle, yapping shrilly and gnawing at his tires.

"Call them off," he growled at Tammy.

"You nearly ran over my poor babies," she yelled, as the dogs circled around her legs and attacked the tires from the other side. "There's no way that contraption is road legal."

"One warning is all you get. We've had this conversation too many times." Phin reached into his basket and pulled out an air horn. He aimed in the general direction of the dogs and gave the nozzle a tap. A deafening blat flattened the dogs to the ground before they raced back to Tammy, howling in terror. Phin grinned his satisfaction and gave them another blast. The four dogs yelped and clawed at her slacks.

"Bastard! They'll be traumatized for weeks." Tammy struggled to untangle the four leashes, while trying to keep the dogs from climbing her.

Phin left Tammy to sort her dogs out. He'd been attacked by her nasty mutts too many times, and would have happily drop-

16

kicked them into the lake. He wasn't abusive by nature, but he had limits.

It was still early as he approached Voodoo Café. No one had brought out the patio chairs yet. The tables were bolted to the floor, but the chairs were taken indoors at night, ever since they'd started disappearing last summer. He was certain that it was tourists, but Penny swore she'd once seen one through a neighbour's window.

Phin pulled the bicycle to a stop beside the steel rack he'd installed onto a concrete pad next to the café. There was room for several bicycles, though the majority of people in town just left them lying on the ground or leaning against the building.

Phin had spent most of his life in Vancouver, where an unlocked bicycle was just begging to be taken for a ride. He put his faith in the security of a length of chain and a padlock. He had just flipped open the hinged lid of the three-cubic-foot cart when a voice called out from overhead.

"Look out below!"

His brain screamed *duck!* but his body froze and he glanced up just in time to see a wooden box narrowly miss him as it whizzed by his left ear.

The moment the box touched the ground one side flipped down and a grey cat wobbled out on three legs. Peg brushed her head against Phin's leg as she passed him on her way to the patio, to sit and wait for the first customers of the day.

Phin's gaze followed the rope that led from the box to the second story window where Mabel leaned over the sill, smiling at him.

"How do you like my cat elevator? Pretty clever, eh?"

"You nearly dropped her on my head."

"It's a darn shame you built that bicycle rack practically under my window," Mabel said, winding the rope around her hand as she hauled up the box.

"And why does a cat need an elevator?"

"Actually, it's more of a lowerator," she replied, pulling the box inside before leaning out again. "Peg can climb the stairs, so she doesn't need elevating. It's just for lowering her to the ground. Say, is that a new walking stick?"

"The cat can climb up but not down?" Holding a conversation with Mabel was sometimes like having all the trains arrive in to the station at the same time. Phin had learned that he had to keep her on track or he'd never know what she was talking about.

"She's fallen down the stairs a couple of times already, and I noticed her limping. She's older than I am, in people years."

"But she limps all the time."

Mabel frowned at Phin. "A three-legged limp is completely different than a fallen-down-the-stairs limp." She disappeared into her apartment with her box and rope.

Phin shook his head bemusedly. He slung two tote bags over one shoulder, grabbed his toolbox out of the cart, clamped the wooden staff under his arm and lugged it all to the front of the shop. Mabel was already at the door and opened it to let him in. He could only hope to have a fraction of her energy when *he* was seventy.

"Did you carve any more otters?" Mabel asked, as she pulled the tote bags off his shoulder. "We sell them as fast as you make them lately and all we have left right now are those weird alien things that nobody wants."

"They're not weird alien things," Phin protested. He'd been tired of carving the same animals all the time and wanted something different. He'd gone to the library and photocopied several pages of photos and sketches to try out. "They're three dimensional renditions of bacteria, amoeba and phytoplankton. It's not every day they get to hold in their hands things that are usually invisible to the naked eye."

"I've never seen my spleen but can't imagine I'd ever get excited over one that was carved out of wood." She rummaged through the tote bags, pulling out the carvings one by one. She made two piles on the counter: otters, foxes and wolves on the left, oddly shaped bits on the right. Each had a little card tied to it.

18

Mabel read one with a raised eyebrow. "*Yersinia Pestis?* Not exactly catchy."

"Actually, it was incredibly catchy," Phin said. "That was the bacteria that caused the plague in the middle ages."

Mabel took a closer look at the blob of wood. "Black Death, eh? You know, that might not be so bad after all," she said musingly. "Might fit in with our voodoo theme." She looked over at the shelf that held the assortment of unsold wooden carvings. "I think we can work with this. We might be able to get rid of them after all." She left Phin at the counter and carried an armload to the display shelves.

He watched her sort through the carvings, muttering "Hello there, *Malaria*. Nice to meet you, *Ebola*. *Legionaire's Disease*? Nope, too long. We'll call you *Typhoid*. Nobody's gonna know the difference."

FOUR

Dee pushed her hair off her forehead, leaving a smudge of flour on her smooth skin. She could hear Phin and Mabel arguing out front. They disagreed on almost everything yet were the closest of friends. Dee wished she could be as comfortable talking to Phineas, instead of always feeling flustered and tongue-tied.

She'd been thirteen when they first met. Phin had been a whole four years older, an age difference that had seemed like an chasm to Dee though it didn't stop her from developing a painful crush. He'd spent the summer in Cricket Lake while his parents sorted out their divorce in Vancouver and then he'd disappeared only to return twenty-five years later and turn her life upside down all over again.

Dee picked up the tray of almond danishes she'd just finished glazing and carried them out front to the counter. It was still quiet but in another hour the café would fill with hungry tourists. She set the tray down and snorted in laughter at Mabel who was sniffing delicately at Phin's new walking stick.

Phin looked her way, scowling at the interruption. Dee busied herself with moving the two dozen pastries from the tray to the shelves inside the display case, concentrating on placing them in perfect rows so she wouldn't have to see his dark brows frowning at her. If she'd kept his gaze a second longer she would have seen that scowl transform into a fond smile.

"Do you think Penny will be on time today?" Dee asked, her voice muffled by the glass that fronted the case.

"She's on time every day." Mabel ran her fingers over the bone and pebble handle of Phin's new staff with satisfaction. She handed it to Phin with a smile. "You're right, I love it. I don't smell the bleach at all. The varnish stink completely hides it, and we know *that* will disappear in a day or so, especially in here with all the other delicious smells to chase it out."

Mabel wandered over to where Dee was fussing with her display. She snatched one of the pastries off the tray and took a big bite. "Oh, Chickadee," she mumbled around the warm pastry, "this is the best yet."

"You say that about every batch. I use the same recipe each time."

"I know but it's like my taste buds forget and then get overwhelmed with deliciousness all over again." She licked her fingers clean and checked her oversized watch. "Penny isn't due to start for another hour. What's the rush?"

"You know I have to take Mom to her appointment in Chilliwack today. I asked Penny to come in early so I could leave in time to get her ready. She fusses if I try to rush her."

"So go now," Mabel said with a shrug. "Phineas and I can watch things until Penny gets here. I'd rather you get Lydia sorted out without any stress and it won't help if you're agitated."

"I am not agitated!" Dee snapped and then blew out a sharp breath. "Oh god, Mabel, I'm sorry. I don't mean to be such a bitch."

"You're not, lovey. You're just worried about Lydia. So am I." She hugged Dee briefly then pulled back and studied her niece's face. She smiled and wiped the flour off her forehead. "I've always said you were made of sugar and spice."

"And flour and frosting."

"Seems more like carrots and granola lately."

Dee giggled and hugged her aunt again, but stopped at the sight of Phin watching her from the other end of the cafe. He was still holding the new walking stick. It was stained deep red and he'd glued bones onto it. The bones looked like they hadn't been cleaned, like there was still dried blood on them. She shuddered and wiped her hands on her apron.

"You're right, Mabel," Dee said. "I should get home and start getting Mom ready to go. I've already got her favourite clothes set out." She untied her apron and bundled it into a ball. Mabel took it from her and gently pushed her toward the back door.

"You go ahead. Everything will be just fine here."

"Don't forget to take the pies out when the timer goes off."

"I know, I know. And I'll put those cookies in after I adjust the temperature for them. Don't worry. I've done this a time or two, remember?" She handed Dee her purse. "It might help to put Lydia in her car coat. That'll at least help her to focus on something she remembers. She still associates that coat with going for a ride."

"Good idea. And I'll pack a lunch too. If I put it in the picnic hamper she'll know that we'll be eating away from the house." Her eyes filled and her voice caught. "Oh, Mabel, what if the doctors say she should be put in a care home?"

"Don't think about that just yet. You have to make this like a normal car ride for her or she'll catch on that you're scared of something."

"All right," Dee said and wiped her eyes with the tail of her blouse.

Mabel was as worried as Dee, but there wasn't much that could be done for Lydia. Her sister had become lost in a fog of dementia shortly after she'd turned fifty, much like their mother and grandmother had, though Lydia's slide had left her placid and staring out the window for most of her days. Their grandmother had been boisterous by nature, more like Mabel, and when her mind had gone she had taken to leaving the house half dressed, screaming rape if anyone tried to force her to go home and put some clothes on.

Mabel headed back to the front of the shop and found Phin clumsily putting several pastries in a white box for the first customer of the day. Mabel bit her bottom lip to keep from giggling at the expression on the woman's face. Phin's hands were visibly dirty and his frown of concentration was obviously distressing the poor woman, who looked ready to abandon her purchase.

Mabel would have loved to leave her to his awkward service just so she could watch but knew Dee would be horrified if she caught him. She tapped Phin on the shoulder and he twitched in surprise and dropped the box. It flipped as it fell, spilling four danishes onto the floor.

"Why don't you leave this to me," she said. "You're all sticky now. Go wash up."

Mabel faced the customer, who was still staring at Phin's back as he went out to the kitchen. Mabel smiled widely and took a fresh box from the shelf behind her.

"Looks like you were interested in Dee's fresh almond danishes."

"Yes, six please," the woman said and smiled back uncertainly.

"Today we have a special. Buy six and get one free, so it's your lucky day."

She collected the woman's money and walked her to the door.

"You can come out now," she called to Phin. He came out from the back, hands still damp from washing. "What were you thinking? Dee would have a fit if she saw those dirty hands behind the counter."

"I heard you talking about Lydia and thought it might be best to leave you two alone."

"Don't worry about us. We've been dealing with my crazy sister for a long time." She smiled and pushed him toward the craft shelves. "Your place is out there, on the artsy side of the counter. You have a reputation to uphold as a carver and as the town's foremost fortune teller."

Phin winced at her words. "Mabel, isn't this getting old yet? I mean, I can understand the locals having their fun and playing at divination, but what do the tourists think when they leave here?"

Mabel sighed and rolled her eyes. "Sonny, this is an old argument. People who attend your séances think they've never had so much fun, and they tell all their friends about Cricket Lake."

"That last bunch was ready to call the police on us. They knew we were charlatans and didn't believe for a minute that you were getting messages from dead people."

"That bunch, as you call them, was two cranky bitches out of a group of twenty. They were dried up old biddies who wouldn't know fun if it came up and bit them in their you-know-where." Mabel dragged the garbage can closer to the pastries that lay in a heap on the floor. She used a paper towel to pick up the sticky mess and throw it into the bin. "I've made sure the group coming this weekend knows what to expect."

"What are you talking about? *I* don't even know what to expect."

"All three cabins are booked this weekend for the first time. Well, at least the two that are empty right now. Half our group will have to stay at the Cot & Couch. I wish we hadn't agreed to let that guy have one all to himself for the summer."

"We'd get paid no matter who stayed in it. For all we knew, we could have had three empty cabins slowly rotting away with no one interested in renting any of them."

"Not a chance," Mabel said. "I've worked hard to make sure everyone who comes through here hears all about you and your talent."

"I've barely finished the cabins," Phin said. "I was hoping for a break before people started renting them, maybe give the walls another coat of paint."

Mabel patted his arm as she walked past on her way to the display shelves. "Those aren't details that weekend cottage-goers are worried about. You can spruce them up over the winter when they're empty."

"It's too cold to paint in the winter," he complained.

"You could put in electric heaters. Then we could rent them all year 'round. It's not like we'll be having a ritual every weekend." Mabel began inspecting the labels on Phin's carvings, smoothing out those that had bent or creased. "Since all we have to pay on the cabins are the taxes, we should be able to earn enough in rentals over the summer to afford insulation and heaters."

Phin preferred the idea of having the cabins empty for the winter, which was why he hadn't insulated them in the first place. He was counting on closing up the three little cabins for the cold season and having some peace and quiet for at least a few months out of the year.

FIVE

Tammy jerked on the leashes, yanking the protesting dogs through the door. They hated going to the vet but were long overdue for their shots. Fritz had tried to forbid her from spending the money but she'd heard that rabies might be running through the area's raccoon population this summer.

She nodded at Ruth, who was leaning on the counter flipping through the latest *True Crime* magazine. It was the only interesting thing about the old woman, whom Tammy had never seen outside the combination veterinary clinic and pet food store.

"How long do you think I'll have to wait today?" asked Tammy. Her four dogs were huddled together in a fluffy clump under one of the two chairs in the waiting area. They'd twined around the chair's legs and were now hopelessly tangled. As usual.

Ruth shrugged without looking up, and Tammy squatted and coaxed the dogs out from under the chair. When Prince snarled at her she nearly burst into tears. She left them where they were and dropped into the chair.

"Is that a new freezer?"

Ruth might as well have been a statue. Tammy couldn't understand why Dr. Leonard continued to pay Ruth when there were so many other people he could hire to run his shop. Like her, for example. Tammy would dearly love to work in the clinic. Not only would she have a place out of which to sell her puppies, but she was sure there would be a staff discount.

There was a sign taped to the wall above the freezer, too small for her to read from across the room. She could have if she'd worn her glasses but they made her nose look huge and she wouldn't be caught out in public with them.

Curiosity got her out of the chair. The sign was handmade and someone had used a different colour for each item. Tammy's mouth dropped open and she lifted the freezer's lid to find it partly filled with fist-sized packages wrapped in waxed paper and tied with kitchen twine, with labels in Mabel's handwriting colour-coded to match the sign. She dropped the lid and stalked to the counter.

"Sparrow Stew?" she hissed. "Minced Moth?" She drummed her painted nails on the counter until Ruth sighed and finally closed the magazine.

"Mabel packaged them up in really small portions but your dogs aren't all that big so it should be enough of a meal for them." Ruth tilted her head and peered at Tammy's reddening face. "You don't think the dogs will like those flavours? You never know. They might like it."

"And just what is *it* supposed to be?" Tammy said shrilly.

"Read the sign. Gourmet cat food. What did you think *it* was, road kill?" Ruth shook her head at Tammy and snatched her magazine off the counter.

"Is it even legal to sell homemade pet food to the public?"

Ruth shrugged and flipped idly through her magazine.

"I'm serious here," Tammy insisted. "Don't you have to have a licence to sell foods in a retail store? How about inspections?"

"Who's selling anything? It says free samples right on the damn sign. Besides, it's cat food. I doubt any people are going to eat it."

"But sparrows and garter snakes? Don't they carry parasites and diseases? You can't just kill wild animals and make pet food out of them." Tammy knew she was getting shrill but couldn't help herself.

"What do you think is in all that fancy dog food you buy for those mutts of yours, artichokes and beets?" Ruth went back to reading, snickering under her breath.

"Well, beef and chicken, of course," Tammy answered, sliding a sidelong look at her dogs cowering under their chair.

"Exactly. Cows and chickens were wild too, once upon a time. This food is based on the same thing your dogs are eating, only Mabel's put a little wild meat in each portion; besides, they're chopped up and frozen. I don't see a problem."

Tammy was starting to feel queasy. She squinted at the sign again, lifting her lip in distaste. "Mouse Medley. You really think people are going to buy a frozen hunk of mouse for their cat to eat?"

"According to the vet it's good for the cats so, whatever."

Tammy stared at the sign for a full minute before shaking her head and returning to the dogs. They whined pitifully as she approached but she ignored them and dropped into her chair again.

Every crazy idea Mabel came up with seemed to be successful. It just wasn't fair.

SIX

Mabel dragged the branch farther up the beach and threw it on a pile of brush. She leaned forward and rested her hands on her knees, breathing heavily through her mouth. There had been two bad storms in early summer, both with winds strong enough to take down branches from the trees that lined their shore. No one had bothered to clean up this part of the beach since most people who came to the lake kept to the less cluttered areas.

"Come on, old girl," she muttered. "You've got a helluva lot more branches to move." She straightened and stretched her back before heading toward Phin, who was watching her with concern. He was easily carrying at least six branches the size of the one she'd been struggling with.

"Are you all right?" he called. "We don't really have to move all this stuff today, you know. We could leave it till tomorrow, or just skip it."

"You're not getting out of holding the ritual on the beach that easily," Mabel countered as she approached. "Are you wimping out, or are you saying I'm old?"

"That isn't fair! I would never dare imply that you're old, and as for wimping out, it's not like I've had much choice. You're going to bring these people to me whether the beach is scrubbed clean or not." He tossed his armload onto the brush pile.

Mabel bent to pick up another large branch but couldn't budge it.

"See what I mean?" Phin said, gently prying her fingers off the rough bark. "You're getting carried away with this idea of a beach séance."

"I don't see it exactly as a séance, but more like a voodoo ritual where we can dance around the fire and try to get someone besides me possessed by spirits for a change." She gave up on the branch and sat on it instead.

"What I mean is are you so sure it's a good idea to hold it on the beach at all?" Phin asked, gazing over the water. "Are we asking for trouble?"

"The positive energy we churn up tonight can only make your job of keeping an eye on this thing easier. I bet it'll do wonders for your nightmares."

He didn't remember telling her about his dreams. He wasn't sure which might be worse, suffering through the nightmares or suffering through whatever Mabel might decide to concoct to raise the protective energy levels around Cricket Lake.

"It's like releasing a valve when the pressure gets too high. We hold a ritual so you can burn off all that power coming from those nightmares."

She was probably right but he didn't say so, instead eyeing the mess of branches Mabel decided had to be moved down the beach, away from their chosen spot. He really didn't feel like hauling all that wood, but couldn't expect Mabel to do it alone.

"What if we used this wood for the fire, instead of moving it just to bring more in?"

"Isn't it too green to burn?" Mabel asked, picking at a loose piece of bark to expose the smooth wood underneath.

"You can get pretty much anything to burn with the right fuel."

"So just light it up where it sits?"

"Well, no. Most of it can just stay where it is, but if I can get a chainsaw I could cut the rest of it down to burnable pieces." They both turned at a shout from the road. Toby had come out of his cabin and was headed their way.

"Oh no," Mabel said with a sour expression. "That old fool tries to touch my ass and I'll fix him so he's only good for a boys' choir."

"He's touched your..."

"Well, no, but he keeps looking at it."

Phin tried not to laugh as he saw Toby slick his hair down with the palms of his hands. "Should I tell him why he's not your type?" Mabel gave him a dangerous look and he took a step back, grinning at her discomfort. "I could tell him he's the wrong gender, if that'll help."

"It never does. They never believe me." Then her face brightened and she squinted up at him. "We could tell him you're my lover. That way he'd keep his distance or you could threaten to beat him up, or something." She waggled her eyebrows at his look of alarm and by the time Toby reached them they were both laughing.

"Hello there neighbour," he said, slapping Phin on the back genially.

Mabel stopped laughing abruptly and glared at Phin, who snorted fresh laughter. She punched him in the arm hard enough to make him yelp.

"All right, all right," Phin said when she pulled her fist back for another punch. "I'll intervene if it gets weird."

"I never say it right and I always end up making stupid excuses that I don't mean," she muttered.

Toby turned to Mabel. "You're a vision of loveliness today, dear Mabel."

Her lips pursed and she took a step back.

"Sorry," Phin said, struggling so hard not to laugh that his face hurt. "I'll just be blunt. Mabel is a lesbian. She couldn't be less interested in dating you if you were a skunk."

"You're the wrong gender." Mabel glared at him. "You smell weird. Your voice is too deep. Your plumbing is all wrong. You'd look terrible in a dress. Get the picture?"

"But isn't lesbianism a young woman's fetish?" Toby asked weakly, backing a step.

"Stop right there," she said, following him.

Phin stepped between them, ready to protect the guy from his own stupidity. "I don't know what rock you've been hiding under all these years, Toby, but you seem to have missed a whole chapter of modern culture."

Toby opened his mouth but shut it again at Phin's minute head shake. He peered at Mabel a moment longer and then turned on his heel and marched back the way he came.

Phin chuckled. "That was fun."

"Shut up."

They watched Toby hurry up the steps of his cabin. He glanced over his shoulder and Phin waved. Toby ducked inside, slamming the door.

"I really should get back to the café," Mabel said, turning away from Toby's closed door. "Penny is there all by herself and Dee won't be back for hours."

"All the more reason to leave Penny alone there for a while. Dee has to learn that Penny can be trusted to run the shop on her own without someone watching her every move." He put his arm around Mabel's shoulder and gave her a squeeze. She leaned into him.

"Aw, heck. There's nothing that gets me more riled up than some old geezer who thinks I'd make him a cute girlfriend. What's wrong with a gal who likes to live on her own?"

"Nothing. It's no worse than me wanting to live in my cabin by the beach."

"That's different. You just want to be near that stupid crystal in case it decides to crawl out from the lake." She felt him shudder and tilted her head to peer up at him. "You're still expecting that to happen, aren't you? And here I thought I was teasing."

Phin looked out toward the middle of the lake, where he, Mabel and Penny had rowed out one moonlit night to drop a palm-sized crystal into five hundred feet of cold water.

"You know, for a guy who claims to not believe in magic, you sure are twitchy about that shiny rock."

"I'm not twitchy, and just because I don't fully believe in something doesn't mean it isn't possible."

Mabel lifted a bushy eyebrow in surprise. "Sounds like you've been giving this a lot of thought."

"Let's just say I'm not ruling anything out."

"So you're just gonna live out here at the edge of the lake, and what? Guard it? You were the one who decided its magic is smothered by water. If that's true then it can't do anything to you from down there."

"Yeah, but you told me we can't just throw magic away. That it doesn't dissipate and would only find some other way to express itself. That it could come back in a different form."

"I also said that intent governs magic."

"We're tempting fate."

"Aw, kid, let's just plan for this weekend. It'll be a fun retreat, I promise."

"That's what you always say, and then I'm the one who ends up playing the fool. I mean, come on. A voodoo retreat? Who does that?"

Mabel punched his arm again. In the same spot. That was going to leave a bruise.

SEVEN

The bell over the café door was jangling Penny's nerves. She would happily leave the door open if not for the air conditioning. Nearly all the tables on the patio were full and only half of those had been served. She couldn't get water boiled fast enough to get the teapots filled before someone else wanted a pot too.

And now there was a gorgeous guy looking at one of Phin's carved walking sticks with a look of delighted amazement, which should have been her cue to slink on over for a chat disguised as a sales pitch. She'd realized early on that some of Phin's woodwork attracted just the type of man who caught her eye.

"Hey miss, where's our order?"

She tore her gaze away with an effort and forced a smile on her face for the impatient customer who was standing in the doorway and letting all the air conditioning out.

"I'm so sorry sir," she said sweetly. "I'm the only one in the shop who's available to serve all those tables *and* help the customers in here." She pouted just a bit and saw the corners of his mouth twitch up while he sucked in his considerable paunch and pulled his shoulders back.

"Well, it's my wife, you know," he said more calmly. "She's in a hurry and sent me in to check on things."

"The tea will be a bit longer, but I have a huge pot of coffee ready if you'd like that instead."

"Sure, but I'll have to see what the wife wants. She'll probably wait for the tea." He leaned towards Penny at the last moment, and Penny kept the smile pasted to her face until he turned his back and closed the door. Then she rolled her eyes and picked up the phone to check on Mabel's progress before she remembered that neither Mabel nor Phin carried a cell phone.

They had helped with customers after Penny came on shift and then left during a lull. It should have been quiet by now but several cars had arrived shortly after Mabel and Phin left. She took a deep breath and told herself to get back to work.

Penny had been in Cricket Lake almost two years, working at the café the whole time. That was the longest she'd spent in any job in her whole life. She had a nice place to live, a houseful of cats that had adopted her and more friends than she'd ever had. She still could hardly believe her good luck and was in no hurry to complain if she was left alone once in a while to run the café.

Penny arranged three teapots, several teacups and a plate of cookies on a large tray and headed for the patio. She nearly dropped the tray when Mr. Gorgeous leaned the staff he'd been admiring against the wall and hurried over to hold the door for her. Penny smiled gratefully until she saw Tammy and her four yappy little mutts at the far end of the patio. Penny hated those dogs. Not only because she'd seen them attack several people, but because she disliked yappy little mutts in general.

"Uh, Tammy, you're not supposed to have dogs in an eating establishment."

"An eating establishment? Is that what you call this place?" Tammy turned away from Penny and shoved one of her dogs around the table leg he'd circled several times.

Penny set her tray on one of the tiny tables, centering it for balance, and tried to ignore Tammy while she served her customers their orders.

"Would you mind brewing me a pot of mint tea when you go back inside?"

"Dee won't like you having the dogs on the patio. You know that."

"They're not hurting anyone and I'm just too tired to take another step right now. It's not like they're inside the building and Dee's not here anyway. So be a good waitress and bring me a pot of tea." She flashed Penny a humourless smile that was more a snarl.

Penny stood a moment, uncertain of how to handle the situation. She knew Dee wouldn't allow it, but Tammy was right about Dee being gone for the day and she didn't have time to argue about it.

"Fine then. Just keep them on their leashes and don't let them bother the other customers." Penny snatched up her empty tray. "I'll have that pot of mint tea for you in a jiffy," she said and hurried away. She couldn't tell if the growl at her back came from Tammy or one of her dogs.

She filled the kettle again and selected a teapot for Tammy. It was shaped like an elephant head and was a horrid shade of yellow. Not only the ugliest teapot they had, but it was cracked and would slowly leak all over Tammy's table. While she waited for the water to boil, she sold several loaves of bread and a pie to a woman who'd come in with three boisterous children. She couldn't help comparing them to the dogs outside. At least the mutts were tied up.

The children picked up everything from the shelves, snatching them from each other's hands as if they were playing with their own toys.

"Um, can you ask your kids not to touch that stuff?"

"They're not my kids. I'm just the babysitter."

"So do your job and sit on them before they break something." She took the young woman's money and glared at her to emphasize her words.

"They don't listen to me any more than they do their mother," she said with a shrug. "If they damage anything you can send the bill to her."

36

A sudden sharp crack silenced everyone and they all looked at the young man holding the red and black walking staff. He rapped it hard on the ground one more time and then pointed the end at the three boys who were staring at him with their mouths open. Their looked at each other in alarm and hurriedly put everything back on the shelves. They then ran out the door and stood on the sidewalk looking everywhere but through the window.

"Wow, that's the first time I've ever seen them react like that. My name's Shelley. What's yours?"

Penny watched in horror as the babysitter smiled coyly at the man and rushed over to where he stood at the other end of the room. She snatched up his hand and clutched it in both of hers, pumping it up and down.

"Uh, I'm Jeff," he mumbled as he tried to retrieve his hand. He threw a frantic look at Penny.

"We're all staying at that new resort up the highway. The boys' parents brought me along to keep an eye on them. Do you live nearby?" Shelley asked and moved closer.

"No, I'm staying with my cousins in town here. So I guess, yeah, I'm nearby." He took a step back, worming his hand out from her clutches and putting some distance between them. He planted the staff in front of his feet with both hands wrapped firmly around the richly stained wood.

"Hey Shelley," Penny called. "You can't leave those kids standing out there by the road or one of them will get run over."

Shelley's head swivelled toward the window that gave a view of the entire street. The children had already forgotten their fright. The two older boys had wandered down the sidewalk while the youngest squatted on the curb poking a stick through the grill of a storm drain.

"Oh shit," Shelley muttered. "It's like herding cats." She snatched the bag that Penny held out at arm's length and winked at Jeff on her way out the door. "We're here for a month. I'm sure I'll see you around." She'd barely cleared the threshold when she started screaming at her charges. The customers sitting at the patio tables leaned away from her as she stomped past.

Penny realized she was alone with Jeff and that he was looking at her. "That was amazing," she said before she could stop herself. "I mean, the way you handled those kids," she continued in a rush, feeling her face growing hot.

"No problem," Jeff said with a shy smile. "They're the same age as some of my cousins. Shock and distraction works every time." He lifted the wooden staff and held it out to Penny. "I really like this, but do you have one that's not as red?"

"Not in stock right now," she said. "Phin makes them all different." She walked over to one of the shelves where Mabel had set out several photo albums. She flipped through one of them and slid the book along the shelf toward Jeff. "Have a look at these. If you're really serious you can have one custom made. You can pick out colours, designs and size and all that."

"These are cool, thanks," he said and gave another of those dazzling smiles that made her knees weak.

She heard shouting from outside and turned to the window again. Shelley was probably letting those kids tear up the place and annoying her customers. But it was Dee, and she was having an argument with Tammy. The dogs were agitated and weaving around tables and customers alike.

Dee was supposed to be gone all day and she'd left only a couple of hours ago. Why was she back so early? Penny wished again that Mabel hadn't left to help Phin prepare for the weekend séance. She glanced at Jeff and then back out the window just in time to see Tammy point directly at her and Dee turn to stare at her with a stormy frown.

Penny watched in dismay as two couples stood up and left the patio, abandoning their lunches without finishing them. She wondered if Dee would make her pay their bill.

EIGHT

Dee stormed into the café, ignoring the glares of the few customers still sitting at the tables on the patio. She'd turned her back on Tammy, trusting she'd made her point about the no pets rule – again – and that the dogs would be gone when she got back.

The café was empty, except for a teenage boy looking at one of Phin's photo books, and Penny who was looking like she'd rather be anywhere but facing Dee.

"I thought I made it clear there were no pets allowed on the property," Dee said as calmly as she could manage. It wouldn't do to terrify Penny, who'd most likely been bullied into allowing the dogs on the patio.

"What was I supposed to do?" Penny squeaked. "She just wouldn't leave, and I was all alone and all the tables were full and everyone wanted their food and stuff right away."

"She said you told her it was fine to have the dogs. You know we could lose our licence if someone made a complaint." Dee forced herself to breathe evenly. She was beyond managing a reassuring smile, but could at least try to act like a professional. She was the boss, after all.

"I didn't tell her it was fine," Penny said miserably. "Tammy said she wouldn't leave and I tried not to slap her or kick the dogs. I just said 'fine!' because she wasn't going to go." She glanced at Jeff, who was politely ignoring them. "Mabel had to go help Phin and I figured Tammy would be long gone by the time you got back."

Dee sighed. "The point isn't to make sure everything is back in its place before I get back. This is a business."

Penny's head was bowed and she stared at the floor. Dee knew the girl meant well and was popular with the clientele. She was part of what made Voodoo Café so successful. Lydia had not been able to keep up her end of the partnership, having slid into her near-catatonic fugue from the first days they'd opened shop. If Penny hadn't been there to help out, Dee didn't know how she would have coped.

"Look, why don't you go out and clean up the tables," she said, and Penny glanced up and nodded when Dee gave her a weary smile.

Penny grabbed a tray from the counter and whispered a sorry as she slid past Dee on her way out. Dee watched her clear the tables and give them a swipe with a damp towel before replacing the tiny vases that Penny refilled each morning with a fresh flower. Tammy and the dogs had disappeared from the patio.

Dee sighed again and headed for the kitchen, stopping in front of a display case to wipe a smear from the glass. She heard someone clear his throat and turned to find the young man who'd been flipping through Phin's display book. She'd forgotten he was there.

"Can I help you with something?" He looked familiar but she couldn't place his face.

"Well, not really. I just wanted to say that she wasn't slacking off, you know?" He glanced out the window at Penny, who was wiping down the entire area where Tammy's dogs had been. "Some rowdy kids came in right about the time that lady showed up with the dogs and she had her hands full dealing with that. And all the tables were full at the time." He smiled shyly, with another admiring glance out the window.

Dee recognized the smile. "You're one of Josie's nephews, aren't you?"

"Yeah, my Mom sent me and my two brothers to stay with Aunt Josie for a month while she and Dad repaint the house."

"But that means she's got six boys for the summer." Dee had been to Josie's house many times and was usually exhausted by the time she left.

"Naw, there's just five of us. Matt's away planting trees for the summer. I wanted to go with him but my mom said I have to wait until I'm nineteen and my birthday isn't until winter."

"How old are your brothers?"

"Eleven and nine. They kind of fit right in with our cousins. The bunch of them drives me crazy and Aunt Josie said I could just go ahead and find some of the local kids my age to hang out with today." He glanced longingly out the window at Penny again.

"There are a lot of teenagers who come around on Saturday afternoons, so you'll have plenty of company while you're here." Dee wondered if she should mention to Penny that this boy was four years her junior.

"Hey thanks, that's great. Well, I should go." He turned on his heel and hurried out the door. He mumbled bashfully to Penny, who managed to look busy while still paying attention to what he said.

Dee suddenly felt old and weary. She dragged her feet into the back room, holding back her tears with difficulty. The familiar surroundings should have been soothing. The shiny appliances, the neat stacks of baking pans and beloved cookbooks were usually a reminder of how hard she'd worked to get to a place where she could proudly call herself a professional baker. But today they only reminded her of her obligations, and that she had to somehow find a way to keep up with the business while taking care of her sick mother.

She had hoped to get some answers from Lydia's doctor today. They'd been waiting for months for an appointment with the new specialist in Chilliwack. She and Mabel hadn't told Lydia about the outing until yesterday so she wouldn't have time to fret or get confused.

The idea was that the exam and tests would paint a clearer picture of what was happening to Lydia's mind. She'd been listless and mildly confused for most of Dee's adult life, but in the past few years had taken to not moving for hours, oblivious of her surroundings and forgetting to eat. Dee would sometimes get home to find that Lydia had wet herself and hadn't even noticed.

The Berkeley women were keenly familiar with dementia, the most notable example being Lydia and Mabel's mother, Delia, who had killed herself when she'd still had the mind to do so rather than fall into complete screaming madness like her own mother had.

Dee had been named after Grandmother Delia and had lived her life in fear the disease would eventually take away her mind too, a morbid certainty that had only become stronger as Lydia's sanity declined.

Mabel often reminded Dee that she was well past the age Lydia and Delia were when they started showing symptoms, but Dee still feared for her own sanity. It didn't help that while Mabel claimed the two of them had dodged that bullet, her aunt wasn't exactly a typical seventy-year-old woman, and exhibited enough odd behaviours to add to Dee's worries.

Dee put a kettle on to boil. She hoped a cup of tea would help her sort out the turmoil in her mind, and in her heart. There were still a couple of hours until the late afternoon rush started. Mabel would be back soon and one of them could go home and check on Lydia.

Her mother had become agitated in the car when she'd found out they weren't on a picnic but were going to see a doctor. She'd begun to scream and to slap Dee, and the car had swerved dangerously before Dee had pulled over onto the shoulder of the highway.

Lydia was certain Dee was going to drop her off at some horrid crazy house and leave her there to be experimented on. They weren't even halfway to Chilliwack and Dee had to agree to turn around and take her mother home. Lydia shouted paranoid accusations all the way home, exhausting herself into a troubled doze before they arrived.

Dee had put a sedative into her mother's tea, her heart breaking as she watched Lydia drink it to the last drop. She'd left her mother sleeping soundly in her favourite chair with a blanket tucked around her knees. She would have stayed home to watch her but just had to talk to Mabel and let her know the visit to the doctor hadn't happened.

Dee and Mabel had counted on being able to finally have a doctor see Lydia and give them some advice on how to take care of her. They had a business to run and couldn't be with her all day. Mabel had suggested a care home but Dee didn't want her mother to waste away in some institution full of crazy people. Mabel had said that she'd make sure there was a beautiful garden there for her to look at and Dee had cried.

She seemed to do a lot of that lately and hoped it wasn't a symptom of the depression that had heralded Lydia's sickness. She'd mentioned it to Mabel once and earned herself a slap on the arm and a big bowl of maple walnut ice cream.

She blew on her tea to cool it but had to set it down when she heard the tinkling that announced someone coming into the café. She peeked through the door from the kitchen to the main room and saw a pair of middle aged women. One of them pulled back the curtain covering Mabel's alcove and whispered to her friend, waving her over.

Penny was still outside, cleaning the patio and avoiding Dee.

Dee came out from behind the counter but the two women didn't hear her and continued to examine the interior of the alcove, exclaiming over the tiny table and chairs, and the pictures of antique teapots Mabel had tacked to the walls. Dee cleared her throat and they turned around with delighted grins. They rushed to her and each took one of her hands.

"Are you the voodoo fortune teller?" the one on the left asked in a hoarse voice that betrayed a lifetime of smoking. She wore thick makeup that had settled in the many creases in her skin and her jet black hair showed a quarter inch of pure white where it grew out of her scalp.

"Come on, Leanne. Don't be silly," the other said, rolling her eyes. "Mabel said the voodoo witch is a man." She was dressed far too warmly for the weather and was so thin that her cheekbones jutted out like a shelf under her sunken eyes.

Dee stared at them as they argued back and forth. She knew her mouth was hanging open and closed it with effort. They ignored her silence so she wiggled her fingers to get their attention and they looked at her hands as if they'd come to life.

"Ladies, did you want to book an appointment for a reading?"

"Not just that, dearie," Leanne said, releasing Dee's hands. "We're here for the whole package." She nodded at her friend, who beamed at Dee. "Sarah and I are here for the Voodoo Séance Retreat."

NINE

Mabel sat in the shade of a three-sided tent, polishing a teacup. She waved to Dee, who sat under a similar structure which was draped with colourful scarves and fabrics over her tent's sturdy canvas. A hand-lettered sign leaned against the table where Dee sat: *Tarot Den.*

Mabel's sign read: *Tea Leaf Haven.* She had decided that it would be a nuisance to brew pots of hot tea at the beach so had filled two clear pitchers with sweetened mint and Earl Grey iced teas. She stirred vigorously before pouring out a cup, ensuring there would be plenty of bits left on the bottom when the person had drunk the tea. The ice had quickly melted and the tea was now as warm as the air.

Mabel consulted her chart, a pencil-scribbled mess of names, times and places. The five women and two men attending the retreat would each receive a personal reading from cards, bones and tea leaves, which meant twenty-one readings to schedule between breakfast and dinner.

Dee and Mabel had to take turns checking on Lydia, so they weren't both available for all the slotted times. Mabel was trying to schedule all her tea leaf readings early, though she wanted them spaced out enough to give her bladder a break. It was a hot day and she'd probably drink plenty of the cool tea. She was glad they'd set up her tent directly across the road from Phin's house – and the nearest bathroom.

A young man ambled toward her tent. His hair hung in his eyes and he flipped it every few steps.

"Hi, Richard! I can trim that for you if you like," Mabel offered as he ducked under the tent's edge.

"No thanks. It's almost as good as wearing sunglasses." He grinned and sat across from Mabel then turned his chair to face the couple by the dock. "Only my granny calls me Richard."

"How's Ricky?"

"Much better."

"Are you all settled in at the Cot & Couch?"

"Yeah, it's an okay place but I have to share a room with my sister and Glen." Ricky pulled a battered ball cap from one of the many zippered pockets on his shorts.

"Sorry about that but it's the busy season. Only other option was putting you in with the two old girls." She pointed to the lake and his gaze followed her finger where Leanne and Sarah were splashing and giggling. "They've been together over thirty years. That's longer than any other couple I know."

"They seem a lot more cheerful and probably scream less than my sister does." Ricky said. He ran a hand through his hair and jammed the cap on his head to hold it out of his face.

"Depends on what they're screaming about." Mabel grinned wolfishly at his startled glance and patted his shoulder. "Trust me, you're better off with your sister than those two." She pointed to the iced tea pitchers and raised her eyebrows. The look on his face indicated she might as well have offered plain oatmeal garnished with brussels sprouts.

So much for tea, she thought. I can't read it if he won't drink it. Mabel consulted her chart and then pointed to Dee, who sat idly shuffling a deck of cards.

"Let's get you in for a card reading," she said, and grabbed his elbow. She tugged him along the beach to the *Tarot Den*. Dee looked up as they arrived and gave Ricky a strained smile.

"Hi, I'm Dee and I'll be reading your fortune today."

"This is Ricky," Mabel said and pushed him into the empty chair across from Dee. She gave her niece an encouraging smile. "I'm on my way to the café to check in with Penny then I'll go make Lydia some lunch."

Mabel knew her niece would rather be at the bakery or at home with her mother, but it would be good for her to have some fun for a change. Besides, Dee had to learn to trust that Penny could watch the shop, especially if they were going to continue to take care of Lydia themselves.

Mabel loved her sister, but wished they could find someone else to care for her, if only for Dee's sake.

TEN

A door slammed and the occupants of the cabin next to Phin's house began their laborious way across the expanse of weeds separating the two buildings. Ramona Hartley was bent over, careful to place both her canes on the ground before taking each step. A younger woman hovered at her side, with an elbow out for Ramona to grab if needed.

Phin rushed to help her climb the four steps to his porch, but Ramona shook her head sharply and he backed off. She allowed him to pull her chair out and she gave her canes to Cathie, who then left to sit at the other end of the porch.

"She's my granddaughter, you know," Ramona said to Phin as she watched him pull a green velvet pouch from his shirt pocket.

"She can hear us from over there. Wouldn't you rather have a private session?"

"She's very pretty, isn't she?" Ramona smiled, ignoring his question.

His face flushed. Every woman he met who had a daughter or granddaughter eventually tried to pair him up. This one hadn't wasted any time. Phin couldn't imagine he was anyone's idea of a great catch. He lived on a beach, and wore satin robes and makeup while he played at being a witch doctor.

"Is there anything in particular you'd like to explore today?" he asked Ramona tetchily. He loosened the pouch's drawstring and poured its contents into a calloused palm.

"Nothing special, though I'm always looking for something that might help with the pain."

"I'm not that kind of doctor. I can't diagnose or prescribe anything," Phin said. "You're here to have your fortune told, that's all."

"Oh, I know," she said with a sigh. "I'm just hoping that you'll be able to see a little deeper into what's causing all this pain."

Phin closed his fingers over his cupped palm. The bones rattled and clicked together. Thirteen bones: seven tiny vertebrae from the ruined remains of a fox skeleton he'd found in a wood pile, and six slim human finger bones scooped up from the floor of a cabin deep in the woods.

"Are they real?" Ramona asked. She reached out a finger.

Phin shook his head and pulled his fist away. "Real enough to tell you what you need to know." He opened his fingers again. The bones made a tiny mound in his hand. "Blow on them. It wakes them up and tells them who you are."

She leaned forward and blew a breath that smelled like peppermint. Phin closed his eyes and stirred the bones with a finger, humming deep in his chest. He suddenly opened his eyes widely and let out a shout. "Hah!" He let the bones fall and scatter on the table.

Ramona squeaked and pressed both hands to her chest as she watched Phin bend his head to the bones. He poked each one in turn, nodding and muttering in a one-sided conversation.

"What do they say?" Ramona whispered.

Phin slowly raised his head and gave her his fiercest glare. "You're not what you appear to be," he said gravely.

"What do you mean by that?"

"There's more to you than your illness. You have a purpose that transcends pain and suffering, though there will be a terrible price for someone to pay." He sat back and huffed out a breath, then scooped up the bones and poured them into their velvet pouch.

"That's it? Did they say what that purpose is? You were listening to them for a long time. It seems there should be more." Ramona sighed heavily and leaned back. Cathie jumped up from her chair and came to her side.

"Not each bone has something clear to say," Phin said with a shrug. "The more eager ones speak up right away, but I check in with the quiet bones too in case there's more to the message."

"And there was nothing more to mine," Ramona said flatly.

"Come on, Nan, don't get yourself worked up." Cathie smiled at her grandmother encouragingly. "My tea leaf reading isn't for a while yet. We have time for a quick swim."

"Are you sure you want to go in that water?" Phin asked more sharply than he'd intended. He'd been nervously watching the two other women who'd gone into the lake earlier, wishing there was some way to prevent anyone from ever swimming in that tainted water. "It's still pretty cold."

"Oh yes, I heard it was cold," Ramona said, patting his arm. "But a good retreat package experience always involves taking a dip in the waters. It'll be good for my poor knees."

Phin watched them make their way slowly to the road that separated his yard from the beach. He guessed that it would take them at least five minutes to reach the water, something he could do in just a few breaths. Not that he ever went that close.

He had asked Mabel to downplay the lake. It was bad enough she'd planned to hold the fortune telling activities at the beach rather than at Voodoo Café, like he'd asked, but it hadn't occurred to him that she would encourage swimming as well. He should have known better.

Phin checked the schedule Mabel had given him. It showed Glen and Tricia were due in a few minutes for a "couples bone-reading session," whatever that meant. He scanned the beach and spotted the young couple near the dock. Tricia was waving her arms and leaning toward Glen, who stood slumped with his hands in his pockets. They didn't look like they were ready. He had time for coffee and a sandwich.

ELEVEN

"Ow, that hurt!" Phin flinched and snatched the eyeliner pencil from Mabel's hand. He yanked his head back as she tried to wipe a smear.

"Stop being such a baby," she said. "If you stayed still long enough we'd be finished by now."

"Yeah, well, let's see if *you* like having charcoal dragged across your eyeball. Dee is a lot better at this than you are. She's faster too." He put the eyeliner on a shelf behind him, out of Mabel's reach. "You take pictures the same way. By the time you actually press the button they're starting to twitch. That's why all the pictures in your house are of people who look like they badly need to fart."

Mabel sniggered and gave him a mirror to check her handiwork. She'd insisted on refreshing his look for the ritual on the beach. She'd said it had to be moodier, a touch more sinister, that it would look dramatic with the firelight flickering over his face.

He squinted at the mirror. The lines she'd drawn underneath his eyes were uneven and one ended a quarter inch past the outside corner. It was also thicker, as if she'd gone over it several times. All in all, a horrible job compared to what Dee would have done, but Dee had gone home to feed Lydia her dinner and catch a nap before the ritual was due to begin.

"It's perfect," he announced with finality.

"You're sure? I could use more practice. Come here." She licked a thumb and reached out to wipe it across his eye.

"No, leave it," he said, wrenching his head back before she could touch him.

"Maybe I should sharpen the pencil to get a finer point."

Phin shuddered at the thought. "That'll just make it easier to pierce my eyeball. Forget it. Besides, it'll be dark and no one will care what my face looks like."

"Are you kidding? They can't take their eyes off you when you start your shtick." Mabel grinned at his expression. "You know I've worked hard to exploit your image. They'll follow your every move."

"The wind's picking up out there. Are you sure it's a good idea to build a fire?" Phin hoped that Dee would be there to intervene if Mabel got out of hand.

"Sure, that's the whole point of doing this outdoors. It adds to the mood. The wind howls, the flames flicker and that creates the atmosphere that allows more energy to get through. Fire attracts power. Pure magic."

"It's more smoke and mirrors than magic," Phin said wryly. "Nothing more than what charlatans have done for generations."

"Are you calling me a charlatan?" Mabel narrowed her eyes and he had to laugh. She was wearing her false lashes and the slightest movement made them wiggle and shimmy. They were as necessary to her outfit as the canary yellow turban and sparkly purple scarf she also wore.

"I'm just saying that a bonfire in a high wind could be dangerous," he said, more seriously. "Candles might be safer."

"I don't think it's going to get all that windy," Mabel countered. "Besides, any wind at all would blow your candles out. We're better off with a bonfire. Geez, you'd think no one had ever burned wood on a beach before. It's a primitive touch that they'll expect for a voodoo ritual."

"What did you think of Ramona?" Phin asked. "She was the only one who didn't really seem to enjoy my reading. The others ate it up like it was gospel and your friends Leanne and Sarah even took notes."

Mabel flicked a hand in the direction of the adjacent cabin. "Ramona's been looking for a magic cure for her arthritis for a lot of years. Most of the others are in it for the fun but she's serious and believes that she just has to keep looking and she'll eventually find her cure."

"What about that couple, Glen and Tricia? Why are they here?"

"Yeah, they're strange ones, eh? Their tea leaves didn't predict any sunny days. Hers said she'd live a long but lonely life and his showed fear of the future and general anger."

"Same here with the bones. I almost made up something happier just so I wouldn't have to be so grim."

"But you love being grim. It's part of your gimmick. Besides, don't you just make it up anyway?" She grinned and poked him.

"Yeah, but sometimes I get the feeling I should just tell them what I think they want to hear."

"Who says they both aren't waiting to be told their marriage won't last?"

"We're supposed to give them an excuse to split up? That's kind of sick. '*Well, dear, you heard what the nice voodoo witch doctor said. Time for a divorce.*'" Phin stood up and wandered to the window. His midnight-blue robe clung to his sweaty legs and he wished he'd listened to Dee when she suggested a lighter fabric than the thick velvet he usually wore.

"You picked up on what they needed to hear and, except for young Ricky, we three gave all of them consistent readings."

"What was different about him?"

"He doesn't like tea," she said, joining him at the window. "I might invite him into my alcove later when we all go to the café for a midnight snack and try him again."

"Why did Tricia bring her kid brother anyway? He really wasn't interested in the reading. He just wanted to know where I got my bones and how I learned to carve."

"Not such a kid. He's the same age you were the first time you came to Cricket Lake. He's even here for the same reason, because their father just moved out of the family home and the mother is still adjusting."

Phin barely remembered the first time he'd come to Cricket Lake, more than twenty-five years ago. It was the second visit – only six months later – that he wished he could forget.

Mabel stood on her tiptoes to peer out the window. Phin had built everything in the house for his height and Mabel was a lot shorter. She could just make out the cluster of people gathering in the gloomy front yard. She grinned up at him. "Here they come. It's show time."

TWELVE

The wind rustled through the trees that lined the shore of Cricket Lake. Ragged threads of cloud raced across a waxing moon reflecting intermittent blue light on the restless surface of the lake.

Flashlights stabbed spears of yellow at their feet as the group shuffled and muttered their way to the heap of branches and cast-off lumber ends. It wasn't a long walk but darkness and unfamiliar surroundings forced them to think about where to place each footstep.

"Gather around the fire pit and hold hands to form a circle." Mabel pushed Ricky between Leanne and Sarah. Leanne tried to fend him off with a fleshy hip but Mabel wagged a finger at her.

"No. We need to separate couples," she said firmly. She pointed to Glen, who left his wife's side without complaint to stand between Mabel and Sara. "Couples hog too much energy and create imbalances in the circle."

Phin looked at the group assembled around the jumble of wood, wondering what made these strangers want to spend their weekend with other strangers, participating in rituals they had only ever heard about in books or movies. Leanne and Sarah were flushed and smiling, obviously enjoying themselves. Glen and Tricia both had closed expressions and were likely still fighting. Phin couldn't understand why they hadn't just gone home.

Ramona had claimed exhaustion and gone to bed early. She'd urged her granddaughter to join the others, and Cathie stood with a shy smile holding hands with Tricia and Leanne.

Phin had nearly called the ritual off when he'd heard that Dee wouldn't be there. He'd never had to hold one of these rituals without her – let alone outside. But Dee couldn't leave Lydia, who was still distressed over the botched doctor's visit.

Mabel squeezed Phin's hand hard, her signal for him to start talking. Depending on the pressure of her squeezes from fingers or her whole hand, Phin could count on Mabel to guide him through their pre-set schedule. He was usually too nervous to remember the proper sequence and left it to her.

He cleared his throat and the group went silent. "We've come together tonight to introduce these people to the great power evoked by the elements of fire and air. Their dance of power is one of great attraction yet consummate danger." He paused and Mabel gave his hand a gentle pinch to signal that he was doing great. He knew this script by heart but had only ever practiced it while facing a candle.

"Fire can't exist without air to feed it, but its greediness can completely consume the air around it, killing the only thing that keeps it alive." Phin winced as he heard an exaggerated sigh from Glen. "On the other hand, if air can move quickly enough, dodging the flame that grasps for its lifeblood, it can snuff out the light of that fire with its simple breath."

He raised and deepened his voice. "Tell me then which is the more powerful of these two elements: the fire that consumes the air or the breath that snuffs the flame?" His words echoed faintly across the lake and he glanced uneasily at the gently rippling water.

Two brief squeezes and he knew to move on to the next rehearsed bit. He began to hum, slowly building the volume. Mabel picked it up on a different note, their mingled tones discordant and jarring without Dee's harmony. She squeezed again and they stopped abruptly.

"Light the fire," Phin commanded in the sudden quiet.

The tiny match flame was piercing in the dark of the overcast night. It painted light across Mabel's features as she shielded the flame from the wind and leaned toward the pile of wood. She lightly tossed the match into the very centre of the pyre and hopped backward as a ball of flame incinerated all the dried leaves and bark on the branches. The group let out a collective yelp and fell back, watching the rolling flame burn out as it rose.

"What the hell, Mabel?" Phin said as he yanked her farther from the crackling heat.

"Well, the wood looked a little green." She grinned at her instant bonfire. "And you did say fuel would help."

"Warn me next time," he growled and left her to help Sarah and Ricky heave Leanne to her feet. The two women were whooping with laughter, a reaction that soon spread to the rest of the group.

"If you could all circle the fire again, we can continue," Phin said. "Follow the beat counterclockwise." Mabel led them while tapping a tambourine against her leg, a pulse that she increased with each revolution around the fire. They followed her, marching as well as they could in the shifting sand.

Leanne and Sarah walked arm in arm for balance, puffing from the exertion but smiling nonetheless. Soon the pace and the heat were too much for them and they stumbled out of the circle, dropping to the ground fanning each other as they watched the rest of the group cavort around the blaze.

Phin frowned at them as he stamped past. Mabel had urged him not to try to control how people experienced the ritual at this point and just let whatever happened happen. Whatever that meant. He decided he preferred indoor séances.

Mabel's beat grew erratic and she dropped the tambourine, waving her arms in the air as she skipped around the fire. Tricia scooped it up and went to sit with Leanne and Sarah, glaring at her husband who had spent the whole time watching Cathie dance around the fire.

Ricky had also zeroed in on the pretty young woman but he was several years younger and she was several inches taller. Tricia thought both men looked ridiculous. Sarah pried the tambourine from Tricia's clenched fists and picked up the beat again. Leanne clapped in syncopation and the two began humming the theme of *The Twilight Zone*.

Tricia stood up and brushed sand off her clothes. She grabbed a flashlight and threw a last disgusted look at her husband and brother on her way to the road.

Phin heard Tricia mutter a curse as she stomped away. The whole ritual was falling apart. He would have laughed but then noticed Mabel had slowed her pace, her arms now hanging at her sides. He rushed to her and caught her as she collapsed. He lowered her to the sand as the others gathered around.

"Mabel!" Phin shook her shoulders. Her turban was unwinding and her glasses were askew. He took them gently off her face and handed them to Cathie.

Phin knew they should never have gone ahead with the ritual without Dee. Mabel always went overboard and he never knew what the hell she was going to do. Had she had a heart attack? She *was* seventy, after all.

Mabel's eyes opened wide and one of her lashes fluttered off.

"Everybody move back," Phin said to the others. "I hate it when you do this," he continued, but only loudly enough for Mabel to hear. Her blank gaze sent cold fingers creeping up his spine.

"*You must be vigilant,*" Mabel croaked in a voice deeper than her own. "*What has been done can be unmade.*" She drew a shaky breath and coughed hoarsely.

"Holy cow, why am I on the ground? Help me up - there's a rock jabbing my butt."

"You were totally out of it," Ricky exclaimed as he helped Phin get Mabel to her feet. She wobbled in their grasp, and they steadied her so she could get her glasses back on.

"She's still not completely back in." Leanne guided them to a log so Mabel could sit.

Phin squatted and scrutinized her pale face. Her teeth were chattering and he took her hand. It was freezing. Ricky took off his denim jacket and draped it over Mabel's skinny shoulders.

"I'm okay," she protested, but wrapped the jacket around herself. She raised her eyebrows at Phin and he stood.

"Why don't you all go on ahead to the café?" he said, handing his flashlight to Ricky. He and Mabel would easily find the familiar path in the dark. "Penny's waiting with a midnight snack. I'll stay here until Mabel's ready to walk back."

The fire had burned bright and hot and was already down to mostly embers. Phin kicked sand over the remains. With the fire out and the rest of the group gone it was very dark and quiet. He could feel the weight of the lake pulling to his left and it took a tremendous effort to turn to the right instead and face Mabel.

"Who was that?" he asked quietly.

"Not a clue, but I'm sure the message was for you." Mabel stared at him intently.

It made him nervous.

THIRTEEN

Penny glanced at the clock again. Three minutes later than the last time she'd checked. Phin had said the group would arrive just after eleven. It was a quarter past and no sign of them yet. She was sorry to be missing the bonfire but found their rituals too creepy. She wasn't sure she believed in spirits and ghosts but it was unnerving to hear Mabel talking with someone else's voice.

She liked to help them out in other ways and had wanted the group to find the café candlelit as they arrived. Now she wished she hadn't lit those candles so early, they'd burned off a quarter of their length in only half an hour.

Penny couldn't believe how much her life had changed in the last two years. And for the better. She'd gone from being homeless and squatting in an old lady's attic in Vancouver to living with four cats in a great little house near a beach. She had a job she loved and more friends than she knew what to do with.

She'd even gone on a date, of sorts. Jeff had hung around until the end of her shift yesterday and walked her home. She'd been nervous and not able to think of a single intelligent thing to say, let alone know what to do next. When Jeff recounted a silly story about rescuing his acorn-thieving brothers from an angry squirrel, she'd impulsively taken his hand. He'd been surprised but smiled and squeezed Penny's fingers.

She'd just meant to peck him on the cheek and send him on his way once they'd arrived at her door. Instead, she'd pressed herself against Jeff and made out with him like some slutty character in a bad movie. They'd both let go of the other at the same time and mumbled quick goodbyes. She'd shut the door and stood in the dark, feeling stupid for having jumped the poor guy.

But he'd smelled so good.

Penny felt her cheeks burn again and took a deep breath. She'd probably scared him off for good, something she did too well. It was surprising that so many couples stayed together, considering how easily hormones neutralized common sense.

She wandered back to the kitchen, turning on the lamp over the desk she shared with Dee. She pulled down several cookbooks she never had time to leaf through during her busy shifts. She sometimes helped Dee with simple baking tasks but they'd quickly determined that Penny had absolutely no kitchen skills beyond making sandwiches or brewing tea.

Not that she'd had many opportunities to learn since coming to Cricket Lake. Between waiting on tables and selling crafts to the tourists, Penny barely had time to think. She'd yet to learn how to mix cookie dough or bake a cake. But she wasn't planning on leaving anytime soon, so she'd eventually learn how to make all the yummy things she saw in the glossy pages of Dee's cookbooks.

Penny checked the time again. Nearly half past eleven. She sighed and went back to the front of the café to check on the candles, hoping she wouldn't have to replace them before anyone arrived.

Since they couldn't move the tables from the patio, they'd borrowed four from the ice cream shop. Penny had covered them with white cloths and placed two candles and a vase of flowers on each, transforming the room into a mystical space that glowed with golden light. Mabel would approve.

She sat at one of the tables and imagined herself in some foreign land, waiting in the dark for a mysterious spy who would bring adventure and romance. She was staring at the candle flame and didn't see Toby until the bell over the door announced his arrival.

"We're closed," she said, but he ignored her and dropped into the seat across from her with a groan.

"I said…"

He interrupted, "I heard you the first time." He pulled out his pipe and a pouch of fragrant tobacco from a vest pocket. "The door isn't locked and you've got mood lighting like you're throwing a party."

"Well, you can't be in here right now. It's a private party, and hey!" Penny reached out and plucked the box of matches from his hand. "You can't smoke in here."

Toby grumbled, but put away his pipe and pouch. "Can I at least get something to drink?"

"This isn't a bar. It's a café."

"I didn't ask for booze, did I?" He took the matches that Penny held out and they disappeared into an inside pocket.

"There's a bunch of people coming and I have to be sure there's enough tea for all of them." Penny glanced out the window again but saw no one coming.

"You serve it all day so are used to making it in quantity. It isn't like you're going to run out if you fix me a cup." He smiled at her tiredly. "My wife's name was Penelope."

"So what?"

"So you're the only other one I've ever met." Toby reached into his pocked again and pulled out his pipe. He clamped the stem between his teeth and opened his hands to show Penny they were empty of matches.

She rolled her eyes and stood up. "I'll get you that tea. You just sit right there and don't mess with the mood lighting." She wondered if his dead wife's name really was the same as hers, though how would she know if he was making it up? She opened a tin from the very back of the cupboard and dropped a tea bag from it into the ugliest pot she could find. Nobody liked its smoky bitterness but it might help to shorten Toby's visit. As an afterthought she tossed in a second bag to make it stronger.

Penny set the pot on a small tray and added a plate of stale, crumbly cookies. She grinned as she came through the door but stopped when she saw Toby rub a hand across his face. She'd seen the wetness on his face shine in the candlelight. He hadn't noticed her and she backed up a step so the shadows hid her for a moment. Maybe he was telling the truth and his wife's name really had been Penelope.

That would mean she reminded him of his dead wife. Sad, but creepy.

"Tea is served," she called. She glided to his table and set the tray down with a flourish. Then she caught a whiff of the horrible tea and felt a stab of guilt. She'd made the guy feel sad and then brought him the crappiest tea she could find. She reached for the tray but he beat her to it.

"Hm, smells like Lapsang Souchong," he said, leaning forward for a sniff. He caught her eye and winked. "Not my favourite, but there was a time when that's all there was to drink." He poured a cupful and took a careful sip. "A bit strong, too, but we can fix that." He reached into another inside pocket and pulled out a battered silver flask, twisted open the cap and poured a splash into the tea.

"Hey, we're not licensed for alcohol," Penny protested weakly.

"I'm just improving the brew," he answered before taking another sip of his tea. He made a great show of swishing it around in his mouth before swallowing and then smacking his lips in satisfaction. "That's more like it."

"No way," Penny said, shaking her head. "That can't be fit to drink."

"It isn't like I had much of a choice, did I? I came into your establishment and ordered a pot of tea. This is what you served me." He took another slurp and set the cup on the table. "I'd be a bad customer if I complained. You might find something worse for me to drink next time."

Penny flushed with embarrassment. He was right. She'd been rude and mean, and was about to splutter an apology when he started to wheeze and snort. She thought he was having some sort of fit when he winked and she realized he was laughing.

She reached out and grabbed his teacup, sloshing some of the rank brew onto her hand, and before she had time to think brought it to her lips and threw back the entire contents in one gulp. It went down about as badly as she expected and she coughed until tears streamed from her eyes.

By the time she'd controlled herself and wiped her face they were both gasping with laughter. "Why'd you come here tonight? I thought you were some hermit who was just going to stay in his cabin all summer."

"Have you seen what they're doing in my front yard?" Toby asked with a wry twist of his mouth. "They're dancing around a fire like a bunch of savages. Who can work with all that foolishness going on?"

"Yeah, this place can get a little wacky sometimes."

"And Phineas with that garish makeup. Too unsettling for words." He grumbled and poured a fresh cup of tea and rum.

"What sort of book are you writing?"

"I'm writing my memoirs. That's a type of autobiography."

"I know what memoir means, but don't you have to be famous or important for that?"

"Fame? Sometimes it's not what you've done but what's been done to you that stains your life and makes it remarkable."

Penny wanted to ask what he meant by that. Her life had been stained from the day of her birth, and had never felt particularly remarkable, but before she could open her mouth the door's bell jangled again and the room filled with laughing, jostling people.

FOURTEEN

Penny finished wiping the small shelf under the cabin window and stretched her back. She gave the room a critical sweep of her eye and nodded in satisfaction. It had taken less than hour and looked as if no one had ever used it, good as new.

She'd scrubbed and swept the cabins several times while they were being built, but this was the first time she was cleaning one after people had actually stayed in it. She'd managed to talk Mabel out of cleaning the two cabins immediately after the last of the retreat group had left late yesterday afternoon. She'd suggested they wait until morning, and the sun had barely risen when Mabel had banged on her door to wake her up.

Mabel had wrapped her frizzy hair in upholstery fabric that transformed her head into a flowered footstool. She hadn't understood what was so funny.

Penny emptied her pail into the dirt beside the cabin and refilled it with her cleaning supplies. She left a bag of dirty bedding and one of garbage in the front yard and went to the other cabin to check on Mabel's progress. The two of them would get the rest done quickly. She pulled the door open and held it with a hip while she maneuvered her bucket, mop and broom inside. She could hear muttering from the bathroom as she came in.

The main room was clean but she dropped her supplies with a clatter at the sight of two canes leaning against the far wall. Penny pictured Ramona lying injured on the bathroom floor and ran to the door in time to collide with Mabel. She peered over Mabel's shoulder into the tiny bathroom. It was empty.

"Ramona left her canes," she said, breathlessly.

"Maybe she had two sets?"

"Why would she bring extra canes? And even if she did, why would she leave them behind? Do we have her address?"

"Why? You want to mail her the canes?" Mabel squeezed past Penny into the main room and saw Phin at the door.

"Aren't those Ramona's canes?"

"That's what I was asking, too," Penny said. She handed the canes to Phin.

He stroked the smooth wood and examined the rubber tips at their ends. "They're practically new."

Mabel pulled off her head-wrap and shook out her hair. It stuck up in every direction and resisted her attempts at flattening with her palms.

"They were right out in the open as if she'd left them there for us to find." Penny stopped at the look on Mabel's face. "She knows something."

"Don't be foolish, kiddo."

Phin turned to Mabel. "Spit it out."

"I got nothing," she said. "Don't know what the kid's going on about."

"Fine. The receipts will have her phone number. I'll call Ramona and ask her myself." Penny crossed her arms and stared at Mabel with a frown. "I'll get her address and send them back to her."

"I have no idea what I did with those receipts." Mabel ran her hands through her hair and scratched her scalp vigorously. She scowled at her friends but they were implacable, staring and waiting.

"I could just ask Dee," Penny said with a smirk. "I'm sure she's got it all written down in her ledger."

"Well, hell." Mabel planted her hands on her hips and sighed heavily. "It was supposed to be a surprise."

"A half-crippled woman left us her canes as a surprise?"

"The surprise part was the special *Testimonial Discount Package*," Mabel said. "Ramona and I go way back. I knew she could use a weekend away from work, so I called her up."

"Ramona works? How could she work?" Penny looked at Phin, who tilted his head and raised an eyebrow at her. Her eyes widened as she suddenly understood. "You mean she faked it? Mabel, that's horrible!"

"Nothing horrible about it. She got a great deal. Now she'll tell everyone about what a great time she had and how much better she feels after swimming in Cricket Lake's healing waters."

Penny and Phin stared at her and their mouths dropped open.

"The lake can't heal," Penny finally managed.

"We can't draw attention to the lake," Phin added. "It's evil."

"Oh come on, Phineas. We dropped the crystal into five hundred feet of water. It sank to the bottom." Mabel pointed a finger at him. "You were the one who said it lost power when it was under water."

"And who was it who just recently said I have to be vigilant?"

"As long as we leave it down there it can't hurt anyone."

"But we have no idea what it's doing to the water," Phin countered. "Why do you think I sit here every day watching the lake?"

"The damned thing is smothered under a gazillion pounds of water pressure. It's as weak as a worm." Mabel picked up her bucket and mop and set them by the door. She turned back to Phin, who was gazing out the window at the still water. "Why don't you go through those books you have on voodoo and conjure up some protection fetishes?"

"And put them where? Along the entire shore?

"Why not start small, like in your own house? Probably stop the nightmares, at the very least."

"The last thing I want to do is mess with something that might make things worse."

"Don't you ever listen, boy? I've talked about intention till I'm blue in the face." Mabel stepped in close and put both hands on his chest, over his heart. "Whatever you brood about in here feeds the energy that floats around us all the time. Good thoughts or bad. They all go out there."

"You think that if we all had good thoughts that nothing bad would ever happen? You believe that for real?" Penny's arms were folded tightly across her chest. "When I was little I wished my mother wasn't retarded. I wished so hard it hurt sometimes, but she stayed the same."

"It takes a lot of good to change a lot of bad, kiddo." Mabel touched Penny's arm. "Your mom was who she was. From what you told me she was a good person. You were the one who decided at some point that what she was had to be bad. You couldn't change that no matter how much wishing you did." She wrapped an arm around Penny's shoulder and pulled her close in spite of her protests.

"Let's get back to the point," Phin said, stepping around to face the two women. "You gave Ramona a discount to come here and fake being crippled, so she could sit in the lake for a while and then claim she'd been healed."

"Yep, sounds about right."

"Isn't that illegal?"

"I don't think so," Mabel said. "Religions do it all the time. Besides, it's like fortune telling. People will pay good money for what they believe in."

"But it's a scam!"

"It's only a scam if it doesn't work." Mabel steered Penny toward the door. "Look, I'm gonna walk Penny home, and then come back for all the linen that needs washing. If you can take care of the garbage, we'll be done with the cabins.

Phin waved her off and headed next door to his house. He wondered if Dee knew about Mabel's scheme. Not likely. Mabel wouldn't have been allowed to get away with it. He shook his head at the audacity of her plan, but had to admire Ramona's acting skill. He had really believed she was disabled.

He sat in his usual spot on the porch and squinted at the blinding reflection of the morning sun on the water. He wondered if Cathie had also been in on the deception. She would have had to know Ramona wasn't really crippled, especially if she left without the canes.

"Is the coast clear?" Toby climbed the steps and dropped heavily into the purple leather chair next to Phin's. He'd brought his own coffee, which he set down so he could reach into his vest's inside pocket. He pulled out his flask and leaned over to pour a slug into Phin's mug before splashing one into his own.

"Do you know what time it is?" Phin asked with a wry grin. "The sun's barely up."

"We're celebrating." Toby took a long sip and sighed in pleasure.

"What's to celebrate?"

"Peace and quiet, my friend."

"Cheers."

FIFTEEN

Dee helped Lydia down onto the kitchen chair. She took the plastic package from Mabel's outstretched hand and shook it open so it billowed into a rounded cape. Lydia obediently lifted her chin so Dee could cover her lap and chest with the plastic cape like a giant bib, and then dropped it forward so Dee could fasten it at the nape of her neck.

"What were you thinking?"

"Aw, Chickadee, it's just a little ad campaign to get us some business." She faltered as she watched Dee's face deepen in colour. Her niece looked pissed.

"Ramona and I cooked up the idea a while back." Mabel moved around her niece to catch her eye but Dee was having none of it. "I offered it to her 'cos I knew she'd be the best one to pull it off. She's had tricky knees all her life and just hammed it up a bit when she came here."

"So that she could swim in our lake and pull off a credible healing and you could get some free advertising." Dee's stormy eyes bored into Mabel. "That's fraudulent. We could get into trouble."

"Aw, lovey, there's no trouble to come from that. A satisfied customer tells her friends what a good time she had. We get more business. She gets a discount vacation. Where's the harm in that?"

"What about all the others who'll come here now, expecting the same?"

"Oh no, we don't give those discount packages to just anyone."

"I don't mean the stupid discount. I'm talking about the lake and its supposed healing powers. Everyone will come expecting to be healed."

"I know!" Mabel grinned. "Isn't it marvelous?"

Dee shot her a disbelieving glare and Mabel tried again. "All right, Ramona was complaining about her bad knees one day and saying it was a shame it costs so much to go overseas, otherwise she'd be traveling to all those healing spas in France or wherever."

"When was this? I'd never even heard of this woman before she showed up last weekend."

"She's from the same group of friends Leanne and Sarah are from."

"But they acted as if they didn't know Ramona."

"Not a hard act for them. They don't really like her all that much."

"So they were all in on it? I guess that young woman who came with her was part of it as well. She'd have to be if Ramona is her grandmother."

"I don't know. I'd never met her before. Ramona might have told her, or she might believe that the lake really has healing powers. It would be more credible that way, I guess." She rubbed her chin. "I never thought to ask."

"You didn't think at all," Dee countered. "You just went ahead and did whatever you wanted to without checking in with the rest of us, as usual."

She crouched so her eyes were level with Lydia's. "Mom, we're going to give you a nice new haircut, all right?" Lydia's gaze was dreamy and unfocused, but the corner of her mouth lifted a bit.

"Let's call that a yes, shall we?" Dee gently ran a comb through Lydia's thin hair, careful not to pull too hard when she encountered tangles. She had her back to Mabel and heard the click that told her the heat had been turned on under the kettle. Didn't Mabel understand that her actions could hurt everyone around her? You couldn't go around deceiving people like that and not expect it to blow up in your face.

She picked up the scissors and carefully snipped small sections of Lydia's hair. If her mother's expression changed even the slightest, she would stop and wait for a reaction. Lydia might decide at any moment to turn her head, oblivious to the pointy scissors.

"Dee," Mabel said quietly, "there's no harm in giving people what they want. We do it all the time when we tell them what they want to hear in a card or tea reading. I've seen the look on your face when you've turned over a card and saw really bad news and then decided to either flip another one or re-interpret the reading to soften the blow."

"That's different."

"Not even a little bit. You choose to give people what they want instead of the truth and you've taken something away from them. What if they need to hear bad news? What if it's the only thing that will help them decide to leave a bad situation?"

Dee sighed and put the scissors on the table. "You're talking about that girl from a few months ago, aren't you?"

"She was thinking of leaving the guy, but chose to stay a little longer because you told her things could get better."

"She stayed and got pregnant so he beat her and left. Then she lost the baby and nearly died herself. You don't need to remind me that was partly my fault."

"No, not your fault at all. She took what you said and made her own decision. Who knows what would have happened if you'd told her what you'd seen in the cards?" Mabel set out her favourite teapot and a cup for each of them.

"I knew she was going to get badly hurt by someone close to her."

"Right. She could have gone home and confronted him and he could have beaten her right then. There's no way to know which way things are gonna go. You thought you were doing her a kindness but probably just postponed the inevitable."

"How's that the same thing as Ramona faking a healing?"

"People need to believe in miracles."

"But it holds out false hope."

"Hope is never false," Mabel said as she moved the whistling kettle from the burner and turned off the heat. "Expectation is what people keep tripping over."

The phone rang and Dee hurried to the other room to answer while Mabel made tea. She chose mint, which had always been Lydia's favorite.

"That was Penny," Dee said as she came back to the kitchen. Her face was a mask of confusion and anxiety, with a touch of anger. "She's in a minor panic, saying she got a call from a reporter in Vancouver from some kind of TV show where they debunk paranormal and psychic frauds."

"What do they want?"

"What do you think? They want to come and film the lake and interview people who've been in the water. They want to ask them how they feel afterwards."

"Wowee! We're famous!" Mabel said gleefully. She danced a few happy steps but Dee's stormy face stopped her and she poured boiling water into the teapot instead. Minty steam rose and drifted toward the chair where Lydia sat. "Tea's almost ready," she said as she turned to her sister. The teapot thumped to the counter as Mabel drew in a hissing breath. "Oh crap, Dee, stop her!"

Lydia was calmly cutting a long lock of hair close to her scalp. The floor was littered with her silky white strands. She let

Dee take the scissors without a fuss, continuing to stare straight ahead with no expression.

SIXTEEN

Toby sat at the tiny table in his cabin and frowned out the window at the boys running and shouting on the beach. He'd counted six of the little ruffians, howling and shoving and tripping each other. That was more tourists than usual for the middle of the week.

It was early afternoon and he should have been up to at least two thousand words by now. He stared at the sheet of paper he'd rolled into the typewriter. Not a word marred its pristine white surface and he couldn't dredge up a single thought to change that. He growled as the boys ran up the road, yipping like a pack of hyenas.

How was anyone expected to work around here? He'd thought he was renting a cabin on a quiet lake where he could write in peace, but instead, he'd been constantly interrupted by guests in the other cabins and by undisciplined brats.

Toby scraped his chair back and stood up. He pressed his hands to his back and stretched, groaning at the ache in his kidneys that never went away. Time for a pipe. He limped to the vest that hung on a hook near the door and pulled out his pipe and pouch. He riffled through a drawer in the tiny kitchenette for a box of matches. He'd misplaced the last one – he preferred to use one box at a time, until the last match had been used. It was a habit his late wife had insisted he adopt when she became pregnant. She didn't want their child learning to play with matches just because his father left them lying about.

He'd likely left it on Phin's porch railing. He'd walk over and check, once the coast was clear. He liked Phin, though the man held more secrets than he even knew he had. It was nice to sit with him and share a pot of coffee in silence while staring out at the lake. Come to think of it, the guy spent a lot of time staring out at the water.

Ah well, time enough to tease out those secrets over the next few weeks. He gingerly lowered himself back into his chair, wincing at the pain that bloomed again in his back. He closed his eyes and breathed deeply until it abated, then filled and lit his pipe. As the fragrant smoke rose in a wreath around his head he stared at the stack of pages sitting next to the typewriter.

Nearly done, he mused, clamping the end of the pipe stem in his teeth to free his hands. He picked up the stack, hefting it and riffling the pages with no satisfaction. A whole life, distilled into a few hundred pages of stories you couldn't guarantee anyone would ever read. He'd wondered too many times whether it was worth it while he struggled to write the next words. But he was on a schedule, and running out of time.

The kids were shouting again – not that they'd ever stopped – but they were farther away and sounded even more excited, if that were possible.

Toby heaved himself to his feet again, grabbing the edge of the table for support and opened the door. He shielded his eyes with one hand from the sun's glare off the mirrored lake.

There were more people on the beach than earlier. The boys were prancing and running around a film crew. One young man carried a camera on his shoulder and another held a microphone.

Toby thought about investigating, but the twinge in his back said not, so he sat on one of the cushioned chairs that flanked the doorway of his cabin and waited to see what they were up to.

SEVENTEEN

Penny wove her way deftly between the tables with her tray, dodging restless children and greeting customers as she passed.

"It'll be a few more minutes for your tea," she said apologetically to a couple sitting at the corner table. "We're so busy we can't get the water boiled fast enough to fill the teapots."

"That's all right. We're in no rush. We're just waiting for that film crew to finish at the lake so we can go for a swim." The man thumped his chest. "I had a triple bypass and my doctor says swimming is good exercise. A swim in a lake that heals is a bonus."

"He's just tired of the pool." His wife rolled her eyes, smiling affectionately.

"Hey at least I'm not dragging you to that business convention in Toronto."

"I should be so lucky."

Penny carried her empty tray indoors. A dozen people milled about, perusing the pastry case or examining Mabel's and Phin's crafts.

Two young women slouched against the wall next to Mabel's alcove. The curtain rustled and they straightened expectantly. Mabel burst out of the tiny space. She was wearing her favorite yellow turban and a striped red and yellow caftan. The robe was too long for her short frame and she kicked out her feet as she walked so as not to step on the hem. She was followed by a thin blonde woman who was immediately accosted by her two friends.

"Well, what did she say?"

"Was it worth the twenty bucks?"

"Should I try it too?"

She linked arms with her friends and steered them toward the door, giggling and blushing. "Shh, I'm not supposed to discuss the reading around strangers," she whispered. "Mabel says it messes with the magic. Wait till we're in the car."

Penny watched them leave as she took two clean teapots off the shelf and set them on her tray. She was glad they didn't offer fancy coffees that took a lot of time to prepare. Tea was easy – just add water, but she and Phin had ensured they always bought good coffee. They ran a café, after all. They brewed and served plenty of hot coffee, but most of their customers were drawn to the extensive tea menu. Besides the usual black and green teas, Voodoo Café offered herbal tisanes both common and exotic.

"Hey there, kiddo," Mabel called. She hiked up her caftan to walk faster, showing off skinny ankles and pink running shoes. "Can you believe this crowd? They're all here for the healing lake."

"Yeah? Then why are they all here in the café instead of in the water having a swim?"

"They're waiting for the film crew to finish getting some footage of just the lake. Mood shots, that sort of thing."

A man and woman interrupted to ask about cabin rentals. A little girl hid behind them, holding onto her father's shirt, and ogled Mabel's turban.

"Sorry," Mabel said and winked at the child, whose eyes widened before she slipped behind her father's legs. "The cabins are all rented for the next two weeks, but there's a bed and breakfast just as you get on the highway."

"I know the one," the man said, glancing at his wife, "but we were hoping to get a spot right on the lake."

"If you want, I can fit you in the second weekend next month," Mabel offered. "It's the best I can do unless we have a cancellation."

"What about camping? We brought our gear, just in case, and could set up a tent on the beach."

"It's a public beach and not really big enough for camping; besides, we hold our rituals next to the water."

"That's too bad," he said. "I guess we'll just have to settle for a swim." He smiled and turned to leave with his family. The little girl glanced at Mabel once more as her father pulled her away.

"Are the cabins really all booked up again so soon?" Penny asked. She filled two plates with cookies and slid a slice of rhubarb pie onto another. She arranged them on her tray along with the cups and steaming teapots.

"Yep, and I think I might have been lying when I told them there was room at the inn. I've sent at least a dozen people there just today and I know they only have room for eight and were mostly booked up as of yesterday."

"Where did all these people come from anyway?"

"News travels fast around here."

"But they don't look like the kind of people who would believe in magic, let alone a lake that supposedly healed someone."

"It's going to be on TV so they figure it has to be true. It's the same as when people flock to some bible-thumping church, hoping for a miracle just because one person was cured from some disease."

"But what happens when no one gets healed?" Penny whispered. "They'll think we're con artists and we'll all get in trouble."

"You need to start coming to our séances. You'd be surprised at how hungry people are for magic in their lives." Mabel reached for a cookie and Penny slid the tray out of her reach.

"But no one's really been healed. You paid Ramona to fake being disabled so it would look like the water fixed her."

"And last year we threw a magic crystal in the lake and completely cured the toxic spill that had sent those developers packing. Since no one in Cricket Lake really wanted to see the beach torn up for a giant resort they accepted that we'd magically cleaned up the poisons."

"But that was faked too! There wasn't really a toxic spill, just some kids messing around."

"That's a lot of buts, kiddo," Mabel said with a grin. "You're forgetting about the most potent magic of all: the power of suggestion. People want to believe in something magical so when it pops up somewhere everyone wants a piece of it."

"So what you're saying is that all it takes is one person to fake a cure and everyone else suddenly believes it could happen to them too. Then why aren't people running scams all over the place?"

"Who says they aren't? It's a big world." Mabel leaned an elbow on the counter and looked over the room. "Isn't that Josie's nephew over there? The tall one looking at Phin's new walking stick."

Penny twitched and nearly knocked the tray off the counter. It settled with a clatter of crockery. She followed Mabel's gaze and saw Jeff pick up the red and black staff again. He rubbed a thumb along the pebbly surfaced grip.

"Why don't you go and see if he has any questions about Phin's work," Mabel said and gave Penny a shove. "I'll take this tray out."

"He doesn't want to talk to me," she said glumly, reaching for the tray.

Mabel gave her a puzzled look, so Penny leaned in close to whisper. "He walked me home the other night and I practically threw myself at him. He probably thinks I'm just some slutty tart."

"He wouldn't come anywhere near the café during your shift if he thought that about you. Look, kiddo, I've done some mighty stupid things in my time. I've learned that an apology does wonders when it comes to fixing stupid. And they're free."

"What'll I say?" Penny asked, glancing in Jeff's direction.

"The same thing you'd say to anyone else who might be interested in dropping two hundred bucks on a piece of Phin's art. Pretend he's just another customer. Walk over and start talking."

As Penny dug in her heels, Jeff turned and saw her. He waved and smiled shyly. Penny managed a terrified grin and walked stiffly across the room with her tray.

Mabel grinned at Penny's discomfort. Mabel had yet to see the young woman socialize with people her own age, let alone go out on a date. The town might be small, but there was a lot of transient traffic, especially in summer. Plenty of handsome young men for her to date.

When the Vancouver development group had changed their minds two years ago about buying the strip of land along Cricket Lake Road for their resort, they'd gone to Minnow Bay instead and taken over the sleepy lake village of three hundred people. Cricket Lake's town council had moaned about losing the sale and the anticipated tourist dollars. They'd reluctantly sold the land to Phineas to build his row of cabins along the lake shore. Now Mabel was out to prove to the council that their town was prospering and that the cabins had been worth it.

Minnow Bay hadn't been so lucky. All they had to offer tourists was the new resort and a much smaller lake which was choked with algae for most of the summer. It was also plagued with more mosquitoes than any other lake in the district. Most of their new residents and tourists simply drove the fifteen minutes from Minnow Bay to Cricket Lake for swimming and shopping.

Dee came out of the kitchen with a platter of cookies. "There are two more to bring out," she said to Mabel. Her face was flushed as she hurried back to the kitchen.

Mabel followed her with concern. "We have lots of cookies, Dee. Why don't you go on home and check on Lydie? Penny and I can handle things here and Phin's due any minute now."

"Tammy's sitting with Mom until after lunch."

"You left Tammy with Lydia? I hope she didn't bring those dogs with her. Lydia might pluck one and stuff it for dinner."

"I can't leave Mom alone anymore and I'm not willing to give her sedatives just so she'll sleep and give me a break." Dee's voice trembled. "Tammy may not be the best choice but she needed the money and promised to leave her dogs home."

"Aw, honey, I know it's not easy but you work so hard here. You could use a rest."

"Actually I could use a rest from taking care of Mom." She massaged her temples. "I don't mean that she needs a lot of care, but it's kind of depressing seeing her like that and I'm always scared she's going to do something crazy and I won't know what to do."

Penny pushed past them into the kitchen. "People are asking when the voodoo witch doctor is going to get here." She grabbed the kettle and filled it to the brim and then set it onto the stove to boil. "I swear I've done that a million times today," she said. She ignored Mabel's waggling eyebrows but only smiled and blushed in answer.

"People are ordering second pots of tea just so they don't have to give up their places on the patio. Some even brought their own lawn chairs. It's getting crowded out there, but they're all in a great mood. It's like this year's festival came early."

"Why don't you give Phin a call and find out what's keeping him?" Mabel said. "I've got a reading in five minutes but it shouldn't take too long. The woman has basically told me what she wants to hear. I'm just going to dress it up in a bit of glam for her."

While Penny punched Phin's number into the phone, Dee dumped several empty cookie sheets into the steel sink with a loud crash of metal. She ran the hot water over them until dense steam hung over the area. She hung her head over the sink, letting the steam wreathe her head and dampen her hair.

Penny wondered how she could stand so much heat. The three industrial ovens were filled to capacity – and had been going all day – and the air conditioner churned at full capacity to keep the temperature in the kitchen at a bearable level.

"Hi, Phin?"

"No, this is Tobias. This sounds like Miss Penelope."

"Yeah, why are you answering his phone?"

"Your Mr. Marshal is occupied at the moment. A rather exuberant crew of young men have accosted him and insisted on an interview with the famous voodoo priest that oversees the healing waters of Cricket Lake."

"Oh," she said with a giggle. "He must be thrilled."

"Only in the most ironic sense. They've had him in their clutches for nearly twenty minutes and are now packing up. Phineas looked like he was ready to throw the lot of them into the lake."

"Nope, wouldn't happen," Penny said gleefully. "Mabel made him promise to co-operate completely, so he has to behave himself. No idea how she managed it but I'm sure he'll obey. Are you going to come to the café with them?"

"Not if I can help it. This place has been like a zoo and I haven't written a usable word all day, so as much as I would love to share a cup of tea with you I'd rather wait until the vultures leave."

She dropped the phone in its cradle and started a pot of strong coffee. Phin would need it. She glanced at Dee, who'd finally turned off the hot water tap and was staring thoughtfully at the ovens.

Penny stuck her head out into the main room. "Hey everyone," she called out. "They're on the way."

EIGHTEEN

The red light on the top of the camera flashed on and the smiling man spoke into the microphone.

"Hello everyone, this is Roland Tyrrell from *Culture Splash* and I've come today to Cricket Lake, a tiny town not so far off the beaten path, to tell you about a modern day miracle." He slashed a hand across the front of his throat and the red light blinked out.

"Ok, here's where we'll cut to the lake shots. Two or three different angles. We'll get some shots of the sun setting over the water. We can put in sound effects later." He pointed to Mabel. "Ok, you'll be the first interview."

She trotted over to stand next to Roland and peered up at him. He was taller than Phin by several inches. "This is gonna hurt if I have to do it for too long."

"We'll be sitting down. It'll be informal and friendlier that way." He waved to a woman who was carrying a dark blue case covered in rock band stickers. She set the case on the ground in front of Mabel and snapped it open, revealing an array of brushes and palettes, tubes and tubs of makeup, and a plastic bib which she snapped around Mabel's neck before she'd even looked at her.

She pointed to Mabel's thick lenses. "Can you see without those?"

"Would I wear them if I could?"

"What do you mean?"

Mabel rolled her eyes. "Why don't we say they're part of my costume and leave my specs where they are, okay?"

"If you say so, but Roland won't like the way they glare in the light."

"I like to see what's going on," Mabel said, leaning over to peer into the makeup kit. "I should have brought my fake eyelashes. They're part of my gimmick. Do you have anything like that in your box?"

"Sorry, no fake lashes. Can you at least take off the glasses until I'm done with your makeup?" She eyed Mabel's face critically. "Let's just go with toning down the shine and leave you natural, unless you'd like some dramatic eyeliner?"

"Forget fancy," Roland called from the side of the news van where he was checking his teeth in the side mirror. "I'll need time to check over the footage before sunset. That way we can reshoot if we need to while there's still enough light."

A crowd had gathered on the sidewalk and street. Dee stood between Phin and Penny off to the side. She wanted to see Mabel's interview so had shooed everyone out of the café once the ovens had been emptied, and had locked the door. The patio had been cleared so the crew could set it up for the interviews.

Phin looked like he'd rather be anywhere else, but Penny was excited and had fussed over Dee, insisting she remove her apron and put on a clean blouse when she found out that Dee kept a change of clothes in Mabel's apartment. She'd cajoled her into tying back her hair, saying it looked prettier that way and showed off her great skin. Dee had complied, not only because it was easier but because Penny had threatened to get Mabel.

"All right everyone, settle down," Roland's assistant shouted. "We're about to roll and the boom microphone is sensitive to ambient noise. The wind will be bad enough so we don't need you all chattering in the background."

Roland sat in the chair next to Mabel's and angled it so the camera would be able to see them both yet allow them to speak face to face. They stared at each other a moment while the cameraman took light-readings from their faces and the background.

The red light on the camera blinked on again and Roland turned and smiled automatically. "This is Mabel Berkeley," he began. "A self-proclaimed tea leaf reader." He turned to face her. "Mabel, when did you realize you were psychic?"

"It's not something you realize, it's just part of who I've always been." She squinted into the camera.

"But there must have been a time when you knew you were different from everyone else."

"Kind of like you with your investigating. What are you looking for here? How would you know if you found it?"

The crowd tittered and the assistant glared, gesturing until they quieted.

"I uncover the truth. Protect innocent folks from being deceived."

"Deception is a matter of opinion in most cases." Mabel patted his hand. "People will believe what they want to believe, in spite of the evidence."

"And what about your lake and the claims about its healing powers? You do know that most of those kinds of claims have been proven false." Roland leaned forward and showed her his teeth.

Mabel flapped a hand and rolled her eyes. The crowd laughed again. "Last summer we threw a magic crystal into our lake and it cleared up a toxic spill. It changed the lake, for the better."

"I heard your toxic spill was a hoax, perpetrated by a couple of local kids." They paused a beat and Roland sat back.

"Those kids ended up sick in the hospital and there were dead fish everywhere. There'd been a construction site at the lake and who knows how many barrels of junk they dumped in the water."

"But there was no proof of toxicity."

"So you need proof that the lake was toxic, proof that we fixed it, and proof that the water can heal." Mabel shook her head and smiled. "Sometimes you just have to trust."

"Not just trusting is my job. I expose fraudulent schemes so people won't get ripped off."

"Aren't there enough religious nuts out there to keep you busy?"

"Let's get back to Cricket Lake, Mabel," Roland said, narrowing his eyes as the crowd laughed again. "How many others besides you and Phineas Marshal call themselves fortune tellers?"

"There's my niece, Delia, but we all call her Dee." She waved to Dee, who flushed in dismay when the crowd turned its attention on her.

"And what does the lovely Dee do besides tell fortunes?" Roland smiled in her direction.

"She's our baker, part owner of Voodoo Café, and Tarot card reader."

"So Dee reads cards, Phineas throws bones around and you interpret wet tea leaves. Is all this a gimmick to promote your café? I mean, it certainly fits in with the voodoo theme."

"We actually named the café to fit in with our theme, so it's the other way around."

"So you offer a variety of psychic modalities," Roland said, ticking them off on his fingers. "You've got Tarot cards, tea leaves, bones and now healing waters. What's next, crystal balls and Ouija boards?" He looked directly at the camera and winked.

"We've tried all those," Mabel said. "They're not as popular."

"So you're saying that some things work better than others."

"Nope. Not at all. Anything works when it comes to predicting the future or telling someone's fortune. If you've got the gift it doesn't matter what method you use."

"Like I said: the cards, the tea and the bones are all gimmicks."

"More like lenses. They help us each to focus our thoughts and energies. They're just tools, no more no less."

"There's a strong Christian community around here. Have any of them protested about your paranormal activities?"

"Voodoo is a kind of religion too." She made a placating gesture. "Okay, maybe not exactly like theirs, but voodoo has some similar practices."

"What do you like the best about voodoo?"

"You can make your own holy water by the bucket full and wash the floor with it. That's one heck of a way to bless a house. My Catholic might be a little rusty, but I remember the church being a tad stingy with the holy water."

"Well, thanks Mabel," Roland said, extending his hand for her to shake. "It's been enlightening and illuminating." He turned to the camera. "Next, we'll talk to the mysterious psychic chef, the beautiful Delia, so stay tuned." He kept his smile fixed until the red light winked out.

"So when will I be on TV?" Mabel asked. She grabbed his hand without waiting for an answer and dragged him off the patio. "Come on, I'll introduce you to Dee so you can get to know her before you do the interview."

Roland nodded briefly in Phin's direction but kept his attention on Dee, who blushed again as he smiled and took her hand in both of his.

"Do you really need to talk to me on camera?" Dee asked nervously.

"Oh yes, you've got a perfect face for TV and the audience will love you."

"See, you're a natural!" Mabel patted her niece's arm. "I told you this would be fun."

NINETEEN

Mabel flicked off the main bank of lights and sighed with satisfaction. She was more tired than she'd ever been after a day in the café, but knew it would be a while yet before she'd be able to sleep. Her body might be exhausted but her mind wasn't about to stop chattering for a while yet. It seemed like a good time to inventory what little stock was left on the shelves.

There'd been no leftover food thrown away today, she mused, glancing at the display cases which held nothing but crumbs.

There were a few items left on the craft shelves, though most of them were pieces that did not sell well anyway. "I spent a long time working on you," Mabel said as she ran a finger along the edge of sequined place mat.

Penny looked up from where she sat outside on one of the patio chairs with Peg on her lap. She pushed open the door with her foot. "Did you say something?"

"I'm just talking to the place mat."

"I guess that's all right, then. I thought you might be doing something crazy." Penny flashed a grin, which stretched into a yawn. She rubbed her eyes with her knuckles.

"You might as well rub the cat right into your eyes if you're gonna do that," Mabel said. She scooped up a tangled lump of beaded necklaces from a shelf. The display rack holding them had been knocked over earlier.

Penny blinked rapidly. "Damn it, you're right! My eyes are itchier than before." Peg purred as she licked her single front paw and wiped it over her face.

Mabel joined them on the patio and dropped her handful of tangled strands on the table. She reached over and stroked Peg's head. The cat pressed into her hand. "Do me a favour, kiddo, and keep an eye out around the place for a little white mouse."

Penny lifted her feet off the ground. "Mouse?"

"Oh I doubt it would come anywhere near us. I'm just worried it might be somewhere in the bakery out back." Mabel sighed. "Ruth gave me a little mouse the other day. She said I couldn't claim there was rodent in my cat food unless I actually put some in the mix."

"So there's no mouse in *Mouse Medley*?"

"Nope, and no rat in *Rat Ragout*. Just the usual cow or chicken."

"I don't get it," Penny said. "Then how's it different from all the other cat food?"

"Pet food companies make all sorts of claims about their foods. They put so much junk in there that isn't actual food. That's why Riva and I started making the cat loaf a few years ago. I'd planned funny labels for the cans, like a cow with mouse ears and flocks of flying chickens."

Penny stroked Peg's soft ears. "So what happened to the mouse?"

"I'd actually been considering putting a bit of mouse, sparrow or snake in each batch and had mentioned it to Ruth, so she gave me a mouse to show me how hard it would be to do. She told me to put the mouse in a plastic grocery bag, swing it around and bash it against the wall."

"That's horrible!"

"That was nothing compared to her instructions for skinning, cooking and deboning the little beastie." Mabel shuddered. "I'd put the mouse in its box on the windowsill, and had pretty much decided to take it back when I noticed the box on the floor, flaps chewed open."

"Peg ate it?"

"I don't think so," Mabel said. "There was no blood on the carpet anywhere in the apartment. Besides, I doubt she could catch it with one paw."

"So where did it go?"

"I'm hoping it jumped out the window and high-tailed it for the woods, though I doubt it would get far."

"We could bring Orion over and he'd hunt it down if it's in the building."

Mabel laughed. "Fat chance. For a tough guy, Orion is afraid to cross the road. He sticks close to home and only expanded his territory when Phineas built the new house around the corner from you."

"Cats aren't all that bright, are they?" Penny asked.

"Tiny pea brains."

"Good thing they're cute." She shifted carefully so as not to disturb the warm ball of fur. "Did we really sell all of Phin's carvings today?"

"Just about. We only had the one walking stick, but we could have sold it five times over." She raised an eyebrow as colour bloomed in Penny's cheeks. "I take it you smoothed things over with Jeff?"

"We both said sorry at the same time and then it was kinda okay again. I don't get it, but at least I don't feel like I completely messed up." Her blush deepened and she smiled crookedly.

"Ha! I told you it would work out." Mabel patted her hand and winked. "All of Phin's little carved animals are gone and there are only two whistles left, though I could have sworn we had at least a dozen out back."

"I brought those out when some lady decided she had to have one for each of her co-workers back home. She tried out every single one and bought the whole dozen."

"I'm glad I missed that." Mabel slapped her thigh, disturbing Peg, who blinked sleepily and buried her head under Penny's arm. "I hate the sound of those damn things."

"She didn't even ask for a discount," Penny said." She grabbed them all and had this weird delighted look on her face. For a minute I thought she was buying them all just so no one else could have them, and that her story of souvenirs was bullshit."

"Yeah, it was that kind of day." Mabel carefully pulled two necklaces straight and laid them on the table side by side. She eyed them and sighed. "There was a moment when I was worried about everything getting too crazy. Here we were getting interviewed for a TV show, and people were trying to get a piece of the action, like they wanted to take the experience home as a souvenir."

"Like the lady with the whistles," Penny said.

"Buying her way into what was going on."

"Some people would think that our lives are glamorous." Penny burst out laughing and Peg stumbled off her lap, landing on her nose. Mabel scooped her up and cuddled her close. The cat hardly noticed she'd fallen and continued to purr.

"I don't know why I'm laughing," Penny said with a snort. "I mean, I spent most of my life fending for myself with no one to count on. Nothing glamorous there." She reached over and ran her fingers through the cat's fur and the purring went up a notch. "Now I've got my own place and a job I love." Her voice broke and her eyes filled with tears.

"And," Mabel said quietly, "people who love and respect you." She plopped the cat into Penny's lap so she could lean over and hug her.

The cat squalled in complaint as it was squashed between the two women and tried to squirm away. Mabel pulled away and gathered Peg under one arm.

"I don't want Peg out overnight and should get her upstairs, but I was hoping to get this money to Phineas tonight. He's always so certain his carvings won't sell that it's kinda fun to be able to throw the money in his face when people fall over themselves to get their hands on his stuff."

"I can take it to him on my way home," Penny said.

Mabel watched Penny stroll away then headed for the stairs at the back of the bakery that led to her apartment. "So Peg," she murmured as she stroked the cat's ears, "What would you like for dinner tonight: Minced Mouse or Sparrow Stew?"

TWENTY

A half pot of cold coffee balanced on the porch railing, flanked by two empty mugs. The coffee had been cooling since Phin and Toby had switched to beer. They both slouched so deeply in the purple captains' seats that no one could have seen them from the road or beach unless they knew they were there.

Muffled words floated in the cool night air, a conversation that could have come from the cabin next door or from somewhere across the lake. Bats flitted erratically past the porch, keeping the insect population in check. Phin had built a bat house next to his workshop and the critters had wasted no time moving in.

"Ready for another?" Phin waggled his empty bottle.

"Always."

Phin carried both bottles in one hand, navigating in the dark with the other from the porch to the kitchen to the fridge, where he was blinded when he opened the door. He felt a moment of panic, certain he'd stumbled into one of his nightmares about the lake. He saw his breath as he muttered his bogey man mantra into the fridge. He snatched up two cold bottles and slammed the door.

The sudden blackness was as blinding as the light had been, and he stood still until he could make out the shadowy forms of his kitchen again. He knew the room well enough not to slam his forehead or bare toes against a jutting corner, but his heart was still hammering and he was likely to twitch in panic at any unseen obstacle that loomed.

Maybe Mabel was right. If he was going to live so close to the lake he'd better get used to the influence of the crystal's magic. Most days he was confident that they'd completely neutralized it, but there were times when he sensed its nasty influence worming into his mind.

Phin could finally see the faint rectangle of the front door, and his first step toward it landed on something soft. And wet. And still warm.

He groaned and lifted his foot in disgust. Orion was a dedicated gift-giver, and had brought many mice, crows and moths to the new house. Phin had once found a good-sized rabbit lying in a congealed bloody hump. When he'd picked it up with gloved hands, he'd found his favourite running shoes underneath, soaked with blood and rabbit guts.

He reached into the bucket by the door where he kept old rags for such a purpose and gingerly picked up the tiny body, wrapping it and using the edge of the cloth to wipe his foot and the floor. Good thing Orion was only cat-sized, he mused.

He was smiling as he came out onto the porch.

"You have a joke to share?" Toby took the two bottles that Phin proffered.

"Just found another dead mouse offering and was imagining what I'd be getting if Orion were two or three times as big."

"A yappy little dog, perhaps?"

"Exactly," Phin said, laughing again. He tossed the bundled mouse into the trash can and set the lid back on tightly. "It's bad enough having a dead mouse squishing between my bare toes, but I'd hate to be tripping over raccoon bodies in the hall."

"Cats are not discriminating when it comes to prey. If it runs, it's fair game." Toby took a long pull from his bottle. "If you think about our evolutionary history, which is really very short, their ancestors likely hunted ours not so long ago."

"Yeah, I wonder when it changed from stalking our children to bringing us tokens of affection."

"I doubt a modern tiger or lion would share his kill with you, let alone ignore a plump unattended child. Our domesticated cat may be related to them but is a completely different animal."

"I don't know about that," Phin said. "Sometimes they look at me like they wished I were a lot smaller."

The two men sipped their beer and looked out over the smooth surface of the lake. The sky was overcast, uniformly grey, and it was late enough that few house lights showed in the distance.

"I've been noticing your new décor," Toby said, gesturing over his head where bones, feathers and oddly-shaped bits of wood dangled from lengths of fishing line. "Wind chimes are generally more musical."

"I glue or tie bones to some of my carvings, and a couple of the local boys have been scouring the woods to find them for me. They bring far more than I could ever use and I'm hoping that if I hang the stuff around here they'll believe me when I say I have enough."

"Is it working?"

"No." Phin knew that was only half true. He'd felt silly dangling feathers and bones outside his door and windows but he hadn't had a single nightmare about the crystal in the lake since he'd taken Mabel's advice and focused on protecting his immediate space.

"How's the book coming along?" he asked, deliberately changing the subject.

"One painful page at a time."

"I don't think I've ever written anything I wasn't forced to write. School essays, work résumés, that sort of thing. What do you write about in a memoir anyway?"

"This and that." Toby was silent for several seconds. He sighed and gave a dry chuckle. "It's mostly lists of boring details and the minutiae of day to day life. Nothing different from any other life, I guess."

"Who's going to read that?" Phin said, then quickly added, "I mean, if it's about everyday life why would it interest anyone else?"

"I'm not writing it for anyone else to read."

"Why do it then?"

"In case I've forgotten anything important."

Toby leaned forward and squinted at a bobbing yellow light approaching along the road. "Ah, that's our young Penelope, I believe. I wonder what she's doing walking alone at this time of night?"

"She's spent a lot of time on the streets of Vancouver. A dark night in the countryside isn't about to scare her."

"Still, a young woman shouldn't be out by herself after dark."

"I wouldn't tell her that, you old relic," Phin said with a laugh. "She's liable to kick you."

"Hmph, she's been spending too much time with that woman," Toby grumbled. "That's bound to harden any decent young lady."

"If you mean Mabel, you're partly right. Mabel can give anyone crazy ideas, but she's like family to Penny and I wouldn't change that for anything."

"I can hear everything you're saying," Penny called out. She ran the last few yards and took the stairs two at a time. She stood facing the two men with her hands on her hips, catching her breath. She tossed an envelope onto Phin's lap. He opened it and his eyes widened.

"You're kidding." He pulled out a thick wad of bills and Toby gave a low whistle.

"Nope," Penny said with a smirk. "There's just over three hundred dollars in there."

"I don't sell this much in the course of a good *week*."

"Yeah, well, people were snapping everything up today. It was a zoo until the film crew left." She dropped onto the top step. "You disappeared right after Dee's interview so you missed everything."

"What was to miss?"

"Roland decided he needed some ambiance shots, so filmed Mabel doing a couple of readings. He even convinced Dee to let him film her touring the kitchen."

"I'll bet that took some doing," he muttered.

"Not really." Penny shrugged. "He's kinda smarmy, but Dee was happy that he was interested in the bakery aspect of the café and not just the voodoo bits."

"I'm sure all this attention will be good for business," Toby said, earning him a frown from Phin.

"I don't like him," he growled. "I'm just glad he's gone."

"Not exactly gone," Penny said. "Roland said they have two shoots tomorrow on their way back to Vancouver. They're all staying at the Couch & Cot tonight."

"I thought it was booked solid?"

"They're sleeping in hammocks. They'll be filming it as an adventure, something about roughing it." Penny leaned back against the porch railing. "Roland wants to film you carving something early tomorrow, seeing as how people really like your stuff."

"Forget it."

"Dee already told him you'd be happy to do it."

Toby stood up. "Give me that bottle. You look like you need another one."

Phin handed it over numbly and waited until Toby had gone indoors. "Are you sure Dee told him I'd let him film me? She has to know I'd hate that."

"Yeah, that's what I told her, but she was all giggly-like around him."

"He's not her type."

"I don't know about that. She went with him for a drink at that stupid little lounge at the Couch & Cot and hadn't come back yet when I left the café." Penny stood and brushed off her shorts. She waited until Toby came out of the house. "See you fellas later. It's gonna be busy again tomorrow and I have to get some sleep."

"Good night, Penelope. Would you like an escort home?"

"No, thanks," she said and smiled at Toby. "The only thing I'm worried about out here is bears, and they'd only eat *you* if you tagged along."

"I would think they'd go for your more tender meat."

"Not a chance. I'm faster than you are." She giggled and waved as she ran down the steps and around the side of the house.

"Charming young woman, though I don't always understand her humour."

Phin grunted and stared straight ahead, clutching reflexively at the cold beer bottle Toby thrust into his hand.

"Good of her to bring you your pay," Toby said, glancing sideways at Phin, who appeared not to have heard. He wore a frown that was part anger, part worry and worked his jaw as if he were chewing his teeth. He had all the signs of a man who'd heard some disturbing news.

Toby cleared his throat. "One thing I've learned from writing these damned memoirs is that as you put your experiences down on paper, you can't help but see your life with a different eye. You re-experience all the mistakes you've ever made, all the things you would have done differently." He glanced sideways and saw that Phin was watching him intently. "It also shows you in glaring detail those chances that you didn't take."

TWENTY ONE

Dee yawned widely as she unlocked the back door. The sky was just beginning to lighten and she was already an hour late starting the bread. She touched a wall switch and the overhead lights flickered on with a hum. She groaned as she saw the mess from last night.

Penny and Mabel had offered to scrub the last pots and sweep the floor but Dee had insisted she'd be in early and would do it then. Those two had worked hard and she'd felt guilty about leaving before they did. She wasn't going to ask them to finish off work she should have done.

Dee filled a kettle and set the flame on high. She scooped an overly-good measure of Earl Grey into her favourite teapot and leaned on the counter with her eyes closed. She was going to need the extra caffeine today.

When she'd finally got home after having a second glass of wine at Roland's insistence, the clock on the kitchen stove read nearly two a.m. and Dee realized she'd only get a couple of hours sleep before having to get back to her ovens.

The kettle whistled and she filled the pot, sizing up the kitchen while her tea steeped. She had several batches of cookie dough in the freezer and enough fruit filling to make two dozen pies. On quiet days she prepped just as much as she would on a normal day in anticipation of busy weekends like this one.

She pulled open the freezer door and tendrils of frosty air curled around her. She pulled out two buckets of cookie dough and carried them to a side counter, where they thudded loudly in the quiet room. She then brought out the pie filling and a covered tray of plain scones from two days ago. They'd be a little stale, but no one would mind once they were warmed up and topped with blueberry syrup and whipped cream.

While everything thawed, she measured out flour into the two industrial mixers, grateful that she'd taken the time to at least clean the bowls and their paddles and hooks before the crowds showed up yesterday. They would each mix dough for several loaves of bread, and she would scrape and refill them several times before the café opened for the day.

Dee flicked the mixers' switches and the ingredients churned and twisted in the bowls. She poured a cup of tea and took a sip of the steaming brew. It tasted heavenly.

The main work table was covered in dirty pans and bowls and Dee carried them to the deep steel sinks, where she left them soaking in hot sudsy water. Everything was thawing, soaking or mixing, so she took her tea to her desk.

She wished she hadn't stayed out so late but couldn't remember the last time she'd gone out for some fun, let alone a drink with a date. Roland had been funny and entertaining, regaling Dee with a hilarious account of a story he'd had to film about reptile breeders – in spite of his fear of snakes – and of the time he'd driven for hours for a once-in-a-lifetime chance to film a restricted archeological dig only to find there was no power on-site and no one had thought to bring extra battery packs.

The mixing bowls whirred to a stop, pulling her thoughts back to the kitchen.

Her kitchen.

Her bakery.

Dee didn't think that would ever get old. She smiled tiredly as she went back to check the mixers. She poked the thawing cookie dough as she passed the counter. It would need at least another hour before it was soft enough to roll out.

She scraped down the sides of the bowls and flicked the switches on and off a few times until she had two giant balls of dough. She pulled up the mixing hooks and lifted out the dough balls, thumping them onto a floured board. She sprinkled more flour and began the familiar rhythm of rolling, turning and punching down the bread dough.

The first rays of morning sunshine crept up the window, glinting off the polished steel ovens and illuminating the flour motes that hovered around her head. She took another sip of tea and thought that, even though Roland wasn't someone she'd ever date again, it had been fun to flirt with a man for an evening.

TWENTY TWO

Mabel carried the box of wood carvings from Phin's workshop through to his kitchen and set it on the table with a thump. Phin opened his eyes a slit and sipped his coffee while he watched her empty most of the box onto the table. She'd come over for a reading but had not liked the look of him and changed her mind.

She was building piles on the table but Phin couldn't discern how she was categorizing the chunks of wood. Only he knew what each piece represented, so her sorting made no sense.

"Haven't you got any finished pieces? These don't look like you even tried," she complained, holding one up to the light to inspect it. "What's this supposed to be, anyway?"

"I was trying for an antelope," Phin grumbled. "It's the third one I've made but the legs are always too skinny and snap off when I'm sanding them."

"Who cares about antelopes? This is Canada. Carve a grizzly."

"I was going for exotic." He pawed through the drawer next to the stove, peering into its shadowy depths, certain there was a bottle of something in there that would take care of his headache.

"Tourists want a souvenir that reminds them of the place they visited." Mabel tossed the failed antelope back into the box and picked up another misshapen hunk of wood. "How about this one? No, don't tell me, let me guess. It's a cat and weasel hybrid." She lifted a brow as she rolled her eyes. She grinned at his pained expression as he struggled to uncap the aspirin bottle.

"Painkillers aren't gonna do you any good today, boy," she said, and put the kettle on the stove. "I'll make you a cup of tea, that'll take care of it."

"No thanks," Phin said with a shudder. "I've got lots of coffee, and a handful of aspirin will do the job." He trusted Mabel but he wouldn't drink from a pot of tea that she'd made unless she could identify everything she'd put in it.

"Well, I'm making a pot anyway. I haven't had my morning cup." She eyed the mess on the kitchen table. She'd separated nearly finished carvings from abandoned projects she knew Phin would never pick up again.

"I hear what people say when they're looking at your stuff. I can tell you which animal carvings they like the best," she offered. She dug through the box for the last bits, and brought out what looked like a whale with wings. "This isn't one that would sell, for example."

"I was going for scary," Phin mumbled and poured more coffee.

"I suppose a flying whale might be scary, but only because it would be huge. They're not really nasty enough to look at. They'd be like blimps going by overhead. Now if you're going for scary flying things why not make gargoyles? That's better than those wooden germ blobs you've been carving. You lose the little card that tells you it's Ebola, and the little wooden blob gets chucked in the fireplace next winter."

Phin looked at her for a moment with his mug halfway to his mouth. "Gargoyles?" he managed. "How are gargoyles more Canadian than antelopes?"

"Each one could be different," Mabel continued, ignoring him. "You could give them names so they'd be unique, like those cabbage dolls that kids used to like so much. I'm sure you could find lots of pictures on the computer to start you off." She moved to the stove, where the kettle had begun to splutter and spit boiling water all over.

"With your imagination you'd never run out of ideas. That would be the beauty of the whole thing. No one would ever see another one just like his. They'd sell like crazy!" She frowned at Phin, who was still holding his coffee cup at his mouth but hadn't taken a sip. He was staring pensively at the failed flying whale.

"Are you ok? You and Toby drank a whole lot of beer last night, didn't you?"

"Uh, I'm fine," Phin said and swallowed the last of his coffee, grimacing at the undissolved sugar on the bottom. "We didn't have all that much beer. I just didn't sleep well." He glanced out the window.

Mabel followed his gaze. "You do know there's no way that crystal is ever going to come out of the water. It's hundreds of feet deep and probably settled under a ton of sand too." She filled the teapot and brought it to the table. It was covered in blue and yellow flowers and had been her housewarming gift. She was the only one who used it.

"I know that, but don't you ever wonder what it might be doing to the water? We didn't think about anything beyond getting rid of the thing. What if it's changing the lake?"

"Like I said before, it's all about intent. We decided to overcome the evil influence and subdue it. We intended." Mabel sipped her tea daintily and made a face. She blew on the steaming brew for a few seconds before trying again. "Ah, that's better. So, back to gargoyles. Does voodoo have them?"

"I'll make you a couple of voodoo gargoyles and see how they turn out. But I still want to make animals, just not the same ones all the time."

"So pick a few favorites and rotate them."

"I'd still be repeating myself. What about creativity?"

106

"Well, la-di-da, what's with you today?"

"Just thinking of Toby, and how he's doing something artistic, for the sake of loving what he does."

"Bull. He's planning on making money, just like you are."

"I don't think so," Phin said musingly and eyed his empty mug. "He's looking for something he doesn't believe is out there."

"Then why bother looking?"

"In case he finds something else, something better to replace it or make up for the loss."

"Sounds like a waste of time. He's just some snob who thinks his life was so important that everyone will fall over themselves to read all about his greatness." She slapped a hand on the table. "Forget about Mr. Narcissist. Let's see if any of this stuff is worth selling."

They re-sorted the piles into one to sell and one to burn. Phin protested about every piece. He didn't think they were good enough to sell, but couldn't bear to burn them.

"Of course you're gonna be attached to them," she said. "They've been infused with your attention and intent. That makes them powerful, which means they're perfect sacrifices for a burn barrel."

Mabel was ruthless, culling the batch and finally settling on seven wooden animals that only needed a bit of sanding and several whistles that Phin would finish later with bones and feathers. She also found two walking sticks hidden at the back of his workshop.

"I don't like how those turned out," Phin muttered when she wrestled them out from behind a pile of lumber.

"What's not to like?" Mabel said delightedly as she studied the length of a five foot staff. It was not so much carved as scorched. "This one is really creepy. I love the way those fingers look like they're burning their way out from the inside."

"Huh." Phin took it from her hands and brought it near the window to have a closer look. "I was going for that exact effect but had decided it wasn't working."

"Sometimes you're just too critical of your own work. Now look who's talking like an artist."

"I'm no artist," he said and leaned the staff against the wall. "I mostly copy other things. I cobble bits and pieces together until they look like something different." He picked up the other staff and ran a thumb along its smooth length. "Toby's an artist. He takes pure ideas from his mind and puts them into words."

"Don't be fooled," Mabel said and scowled at him. "He's just writing about things that have happened to him. Doesn't make him an artist, more like a reporter."

"At least he's enjoying himself."

"He's just a grumpy old geezer."

"Funny, that's exactly how he describes you…ouch!" Phin couldn't quite suppress a snort of laughter as she punched his arm. "You're feisty for an old geezer."

"All right, smart guy. I'll make you another pot of coffee if you finish some of these so I've got something to put on the shelves today."

"Fine. I'll start sanding." He sat at the table pretending to sand, but watched Mabel's every move. He didn't think she could do anything too crazy to a pot of coffee, but he'd known her too long not to be wary.

"So, I hear Dee went out with that guy," he said quietly while he watched her measure coffee into a filter. It was going to be a strong brew, judging by her cavalier scooping. Phin approved.

"Yeah, but I haven't spoken to her about it yet. He's kinda cute."

"How would you know?"

"Hey! Just because I don't swing that way doesn't mean I can't admire a cute butt." She pressed the switch and the coffee maker began its gurgling cycle. "Besides, I don't see *you* making any moves."

TWENTY THREE

Penny wove her way through the crowded room, maneuvering her tray over customers' heads without spilling a drop or losing a single cookie. She paused as a man opened the door, and slid through when he held it for her. There were people at every table on the patio and several waved for her attention. She smiled at them and quickly emptied her tray of teapots, cups and plates. She scooped up coins and crumpled bills from empty tables as she passed, and filled her tray again with dirty dishes.

"Hey Penny!" Jeff leaped up the four steps to the patio in one bound and was grinning in her face before she had a chance to register that her name had been called.

"H-hi," she stammered. He was standing so close that it made her dizzy to look up at him. She took a step back and kept a tight grip on her tray.

"A bunch of us are going to the lake later for a swim. Want to come?"

"I'm closing tonight. What time are you going?" She felt a stab of panic. What did he mean by a bunch? And there was no way she'd ever swim in that lake.

"Not till after dark. We want to have a fire. I saw one there last weekend. My Aunt Josie said it wasn't allowed, but I'm thinking she made that up. It's her default position whenever my cousins come up with some scheme they want to try." He laughed a deep easy chuckle that made Penny's knees tremble.

"I should have everything cleaned up and the cash done by then. Where's it going to be? Will I know anyone?"

"Sure, you'll know Mellie and Dave at least."

"Aren't they a couple?"

"Naw, they just hang out together a lot. They invited some friends from Minnow Bay too, and they might bring a few others." He touched her arm. "Come on, it'll be fun."

Penny's arm was on fire where his fingers touched it. Her throat felt so tight she didn't think she'd be able to talk, but she opened her mouth anyway. "Um, ok. I'll want to go home and change first."

"Meet us at the pier at sunset. We're going to walk partway around the west side of the lake for some privacy. That way we won't have someone calling the cops or coming over to tell us to put the fire out."

He was gone in a flash, walking toward the beer store. He turned once and lifted a hand. Penny managed a limp wave.

Penny carried her laden tray into the café, where Roland and his film crew were gathered around the glass display case Dee had just filled with fresh cherry scones and several varieties of cookies.

"We'll need coffee to go," one of the crew barked as Penny shouldered her way past them.

"We don't have coffee to go," Dee retorted as she filled a bag with cookies. "We don't use disposable cups."

"How are we supposed to take coffee with us? We're running late and have to shoot for two other shows on the way back to Vancouver."

"Unless you brought a thermos, you'll have to drink it here or see if the gas station has anything fresher than day before yesterday's."

Penny tuned them out and continued through the doorway to the fridge. She poured a tall glass of lemonade and swallowed it in two gulps, pressing her fingers against her temples when the icy drink threatened to give her a headache.

Could she really go to the beach with Jeff and his friends? Had he told them how she'd behaved when he'd walked her home? She hadn't had many friends before her mother got killed when she was ten. Any kids who did talk to her just wanted to know what it was like to have a retard for a mom. Her Aunt Margaret hadn't put much energy into taking care of her niece, so Penny mostly raised herself.

"Come on, girl, you can do this," she muttered as she went back out front to help Dee. She could hear Mabel bossing Phin around over the noise in the room.

"Don't put those on the top shelf. No one will see them way up there."

"Only if they're as short as you," Phin growled. "The top shelf is just about eye level for most people. You don't want the little kids to be able to reach these whistles, do you?"

Mabel made a face. "Okay, okay, point made. But spread things out a little bit so it'll look like there's more on the shelf."

"Spread them out all you want but they're still only a handful. So we don't have much to sell right now. Big deal. It just shows how well we've been doing."

Phin glanced at Dee, who stood next to the cash register. She had a smudge of yellow icing on her cheek and flour dusted her bangs. Roland was talking to her, leaning across the counter intimately. She smiled at something he said but the smile disappeared when she noticed Phin watching them.

He scowled as he turned away and knocked over his two walking sticks. They hit the floor with a loud clatter, drawing everyone's attention and silencing the room. He picked them up, cursing under his breath as he leaned the staves against a shelf and checked them for damage. He tapped pebbles and bones to ensure they were still solidly glued to the wood, and nearly knocked them over again when a heavy hand landed on his shoulder. He shrugged it off and turned around.

"Hey, witch doctor," Roland said with a wide smile that didn't reach his eyes. "How about you pose next to your crafts? I could use a few more shots to give my footage that quaint feel."

"I've got some new tea cozies over here too," Mabel said and stepped up to face Roland. She grinned and pointed to a shelf of crocheted and quilted covers.

He ignored her and spoke to Phin over her head. "I need some footage that will save the show if the whole voodoo shtick bombs."

"No thanks." Phin pushed his way past Roland, shaking his head sharply at the camera-wielding woman who stood next to him.

"This isn't good for your image," Roland said, following him. "You could use the exposure."

Phin stopped abruptly and Roland bumped into him. "Look," he said a little too loudly, "you've had your fun. Now take your crew and go home." He glanced over at Dee, who was staring, and felt his stomach drop as he realized the whole room was watching. He was causing a scene and embarrassing Dee. What harm could it do to let the guy take a few more shots? Maybe then he'd get the hell out of Cricket Lake and let them all get back to their lives. He turned back to Roland, who'd followed Phin's line of sight.

"I wouldn't bother with that one," Roland said with a smirk. "I couldn't even get to first base."

Roland hadn't lowered his voice and Phin was sure Dee had heard every word, a fear that was confirmed when he looked back her way. She was still flushed a deep pink but now her mouth was slightly open in surprise and dismay.

Phin seethed with anger and would have flattened Roland, but was more concerned about getting to Dee. He shoved past several people, and others stepped out of his path quickly. He rounded the corner of the counter and walked straight to her. Up close he could see she was on the brink of tears. He thought she had never looked so beautiful, and couldn't believe he'd let Roland get close enough to hurt her.

He wiped the icing from her cheek with a thumb and pressed his palm to her warm skin. "Do you trust me?" he asked hoarsely.

Dee trembled as her eyes searched his, and a tear escaped and rolled onto his hand. He barely heard her whisper, "Yes."

Phin's heart raced, and he felt his mouth go dry. The room was filled with chatter that he only dimly heard as his focus narrowed and he knew only Dee.

"I'm going to kiss you now," he mumbled and leaned forward. Her eyes closed the moment his lips touched hers, and he thought he had never felt anything so soft. It was over too soon and he might not have believed it had actually happened except for Dee's tender smile.

"Wow, it's about time," Mabel said from the other side of the counter, beaming a happy smile at Dee and Phin. "But Roland is leaving without his extra footage. Do you want me to chase him down for more pictures?" Her grin widened when Phin frowned at her.

"I didn't think so," she said smugly as the café's door closed behind Roland and his crew.

TWENTY FOUR

The sun was high and hot. Phin kept his head down as his feet trod the familiar path home. His mood swung between elation and panic, and he could hardly catch his breath.

He'd kissed Dee. She'd kissed him back. She had returned his kiss with her hand pressed against his chest before she'd run off to hide in the kitchen when she realized everyone was watching.

Mabel and Penny had giggled like schoolgirls, causing Phin to finally make his own escape from their teasing. At least the kiss had the effect he'd hoped for: Roland rounded up his crew and left town immediately.

He had to keep reminding himself of the reality of it, though that kiss was so deeply implanted in his soul there was no way he'd ever forget it. For most of his adult life he'd never allowed himself the luxury of being with a woman he cared for, and wasn't certain he knew what to do next.

He wondered if he'd done the right thing. His whole life was a testament to how the simplest action can initiate a disastrous event. Had he been too rash? Would Dee now avoid him, embarrassed by his territorial caveman behavior?

He'd been in Cricket Lake for two years, and in all that time he'd never made any move to show her how he felt. She'd been skittish, wrapped up in her own problems and fears, so he'd simply been her friend. He'd grown comfortable around her, and believed he had all the time in the world.

What changed? It wasn't just Roland; men often flirted with Dee at the bakery. There was something sensual about someone who spent her days baking comfort foods. He'd learned to ignore the attention they paid her. It wasn't his business who she talked to.

Phin halted and surveyed his house and its neighbouring cabins. He wished he could have built his house a lot farther down Cricket Lake Road. There was no need for him to be so close to the cabins, except that the town council had only approved construction of his four structures on the one plot of land. Phin neglected to mention that one of the cabins would be much larger and house a permanent resident. No one had complained.

On hot days when the beach was too crowded for his liking, he sat on the smaller porch that led from the back door into his workshop. He was grateful to Fritz for suggesting, when they drew up the building plans, that they extend the back of the house another fifteen feet to include a shop and a veranda for outdoor work. It was invisible from the beach and main road so no one who didn't know it was there ever came to visit when he was working.

Phin ran his gaze over the three identical cabins to the last one in the row. He wondered if Toby was writing and whether he should disturb him. He knew how annoying it could be to have someone suddenly appear and snap the creative energy off right in the middle of a brilliant burst of genius.

Toby had said that one of the best things about writing his memoirs was that he could revisit all the great moments of his life, though it also highlighted the chances he hadn't had the courage to take.

Was that what had spurred Phin's impulse to finally kiss Dee? He could probably come up with a dozen times where he'd thought of telling her how he felt. But he'd always resisted those urges before today, telling himself that she deserved better. He'd resisted his feelings to save her from grief.

Phin wondered what chances Toby hadn't taken in his life. He'd seemed wistful as he'd made the comment, as if regret had faded over time only to resurface when he started to sift through memories and sort them into his chronicle.

To hell with worrying about disturbing his precious work, Phin thought with a grin. He wanted to thank Toby for his insight and to share the results. He ran the last few steps, landing on the cabin's low porch with enough noise to announce his presence.

"Hey old man," he shouted as he pounded on the door. "Time for a break. Pack your pipe and come sit outside in the sun before you miss the whole day."

Phin pressed an ear to the door, listening for the tapping of the typewriter's keys, but heard nothing. He shoved his hands into his pockets and leaned on the cabin wall, scanning the beach for the older man. It wasn't like Toby to venture out during daylight, as he usually spent those hours pounding away on his typewriter. He hated running into nosy neighbors or having to deal with kids racing around. It was one of the things he and Phin had in common.

He was probably having a nap, Phin thought as he turned back to give the door a few more thumps. That's when he glimpsed the back of Toby' head through the window. He cupped his hands around his eyes to cut the glare and peered through the glass, squinting to focus past the lace curtains Mabel had insisted on hanging.

The old man had fallen asleep at the typewriter and was slumped in his chair. He must have worked through the night, Phin thought, and would have a sore neck from sleeping with his chin on his chest. All the more reason to wake him.

Phin tried the door and found it unlocked. He walked in, feeling mildly foolish for barging in on the man, but a nagging voice at the back of his mind wondered how all the noise he'd made hadn't woken Toby by now.

The smell hit him just as he kicked a bottle that lay in his path, sending it spinning across the floor with an over-loud clink in the stifling room. An icy sweat broke out on his scalp as the bottle landed in a puddle of pale liquid under the chair that could have been either whisky or urine.

Time slowed as he dragged his eyes from the bottle up to Toby' slack grey face. His left hand lay on a stack of paper and there was a faint smile on his lips. There was a smaller bottle standing nearby, cap off and empty. Phin nearly bolted from the room as his mind added up all the clues: pills, booze and a lifeless body.

"Hey, old man," he whispered, and forced a shaking hand to his friend's throat to check for a pulse, pulling it back when he felt only cold, waxy skin. "Damn it, Toby," he tried again, shoving his shoulder gently. He met a stiff resistance that a lifetime of TV crime shows informed him was rigor mortis. How long had he been dead, and had he been growing cold while Phin was seizing his opportunity with Dee?

His eyes moved to the ancient typewriter. It held a page with two words, centred: *The End.*

So Toby had finally finished his book. Had he come to Cricket Lake intending to kill himself after he'd completed it? Phin raked his fingers through his hair, wondering what he should do. The police would have to be called. He knew Toby didn't have any family to contact.

He glanced at the table again. Everything was quite orderly. The stack of paper that must be the manuscript sat to the left of the typewriter, and three envelopes lined up on the right. Phin closed his eyes when he saw his name written on one envelope.

He reached a hand out blindly and grabbed it, forcing himself not to crush the paper. He took several calming breaths before opening his eyes again to read the names on the other two envelopes. There was one for Penny, though it was addressed to *My Dear Penelope*, and the other was simply labeled *suicide note.*

Phin laughed aloud at that, though it was a strangled sound that ended almost in a whimper. Leave it to a writer to not only carefully stage his own death, but to stage-direct the aftermath.

He took his letter outside and sat on a lawn chair. Children screamed in the distance as they chased a dog that had stolen their frisbee, and a couple strolled hand in hand along the shore. They leaned toward each other as if to share a secret and Phin heard the woman laugh, unaware of the tragedy within shouting distance.

Phin gripped the envelope in both hands and stared at his name printed in shaky script. Had Toby already taken his fatal dose when he sealed the envelope? A spark of anger almost made him tear the envelope to shreds without reading what was inside, but curiosity won and he slid a finger under the flap to break the seal. He would read it first and then call the police. He pulled out a single typed page and unfolded it.

"Phineas, my friend," it began. *"I trust that I can still call you friend, even though I've selfishly left you with the burden of my remains. I had not hoped to meet one such as you, a man who had only just learned how to live his life, beginning as if from the start but with the wisdom of experience.*

"I've never had that privilege, having married young and been blessed with five blissful years before losing my Penelope while she birthed our stillborn son. She was the love of my life, a life that was over before it properly began. Mine ended on the same day, though I trudged through the years vainly looking for a way to join her without bringing shame to her memory.

"I thought I'd managed it once, foolishly making a devil's deal that should have saved many, but my bold gesture floundered and failed, bringing only more death and pain. Now a new pain haunts me, one they can't do anything about. I thought I'd have more time.

"I'll leave off here, saying only that you must give the manuscript to our young Penny. Her letter contains instructions as well as more apologies.

"Remember to seize that which will bring you happiness. You know what I mean and my most fervent wish is that you will have more courage than I have been able to muster."

TWENTY FIVE

Penny sat on Phin's porch in his purple captain's chair. On her lap was a box from his woodshop. Sawdust still clung to the cardboard sides and stuck to her fingers when she brushed it away. She riffled the pages that nearly filled the box and a whiff of Toby's pipe smoke rose from the manuscript.

"Hey kiddo," Mabel said as she dropped into the other chair. She looked smaller than usual as she slumped with her feet sticking straight out. "That's the ambulance gone finally."

"I feel sick." Penny's face was blotchy with tears. "I was planning to go out and have a good time while he was here dying. He was all alone." She hiccupped and wiped fresh tears with her sleeve.

"We all die alone," Mabel said flatly. "He just chose when it would happen. You heard that policeman. The suicide note said that Toby had only a couple of months to live. He didn't want to spend them in a hospital, so doped up on morphine he wouldn't even be aware he was dying."

"He never mentioned he was sick."

"He didn't tell anybody. He was probably in a lot of pain, judging from the small pharmacy in his bathroom."

"Couldn't he get help?" Penny sniffed loudly.

"Hardly any cancers are curable. I think they can slow some of them down but sometimes the treatment is more deadly than the disease." She ran a finger along the edge of the box and Penny clutched it more tightly. "Don't worry. I certainly don't want it. I'm not even sure I'll want to read the damn thing."

"I'm going to stay up all night and read it," Penny said hollowly. She turned to face Mabel. "He wants me to find some publisher and make it into a book. He even gave me a name to call. His letter said the world had to know what he'd done."

"You sure you want to know tonight?"

"Not really. But it's creepy enough having this box of paper that a dead guy wrote without knowing what's on the pages. I mean, what if it's something really bad the police need to know about?"

"I doubt he's got a bunch of bodies stashed in some field."

"Don't say that!" Penny shuddered and swallowed a few times. "I feel like I might throw up."

"You need some water."

"What I need is strong coffee."

"Phineas will have some. Let's go inside."

"It's too close." Penny got to her feet while clutching the heavy box to her chest. "It's creepy out here. Come home with me and I'll make a pot."

"Sure, kiddo, but it's way too late for this old gal to be drinking coffee."

"I have decaf."

Penny waited on the road while Mabel locked up Phin's house and left a light on for him. It would be fully dark by the time he got back from Dee's house. He'd left as soon as Penny had arrived after closing the café early, only taking a moment to thrust the box of paper in her arms. Mabel had dealt with the police and paramedics while Penny had sat on Phin's porch, cradling the box.

The sun had set at least an hour ago and the way was gloomy so they kept their eyes on the small yellow circle Mabel's flashlight made on the road to Penny's house.

A small shadow detached from the base of a tree and fell into place beside the women, padding silently. A second shadow crashed out of the darkness moments later. Hercules butted his head against Orion's and ran ahead, leading the way to dinner.

"Do you think the cabin's haunted now?" Penny asked quietly.

"I hope so," Mabel said. "The tourists will eat it up. We could probably hold séances in it, though it's pretty small."

"Oh come on! Someone died in there."

"I know," Mabel said and put an arm around Penny's trembling shoulders. "I think that's why he came here."

"To kill himself?"

"Well, to finish his book, I guess, but yeah, I think he came here to die."

"Why would he come here?"

"Oh, we were probably the only place that had a cabin available for a couple of months. It could have been anywhere. It was just chance that led him here."

Penny peered at Mabel's face in the gloom. "You don't believe that. I can see it in your eyes."

"How many other people do you know that have the same name as you do?"

"I've never met anyone else named Penny, but you can't think that he knew there was someone here with his dead wife's name."

"Didn't need to. Don't you remember that reading you had last fall that said you'd finally meet someone who'd been looking for you all his life?"

"I thought that meant I'd finally meet the man of my dreams."

"Sometimes we misinterpret the message. Toby has been waiting to die so he could be reunited with his Penelope."

"But what's that got to do with me?" Penny shivered in the cool evening air.

"Maybe you were just a sign for him that he'd found the right place to be, and that you were the one person he could trust to tie up this one loose end."

"A stupid book about how he's been waiting to join his dead wife. Great. Should be a fascinating read."

"I think you'll be surprised by what you find." Mabel ran lightly up the front steps of Penny's house, Orion and Hercules crowding her through the front door. She led them to the kitchen, flicking on all the lights as she went.

Penny trudged behind with the box, trying not to trip on the two identical orange cats that wound around her legs.

"They're not as fat as when Phineas lived here," Mabel said, petting Castor and Pollux while Penny thawed a packet of Minced Mouse in the microwave.

"I hated when they left food on the plate to eat later. It smelled disgusting and I didn't want to clean up the dried guck they didn't eat. So I just gave them a bit less each time until they finished the whole meal in one sitting." She dumped the food onto a plate and broke it into smaller chunks. She smiled as the cats devoured the food and licked the plate clean.

"Good to see you smile, kiddo," Mabel said as she set a kettle on the stove. "You got anything for hungry humans too?"

"There's lots in the freezer, but the labels keep falling off so I mostly guess by color and shape." Penny dropped into a chair and peered into the box she'd left on the floor. "*A Life Hardly Lived*. By Tobias Greer."

"Doesn't sound like such an exciting life."

"Couldn't have been too boring if he managed to fill up so many pages." Mabel popped a container in the microwave and pulled two plates off a shelf. "He was a journalist and traveled all over the world, so he probably saw some really interesting history happen."

"So. He could have reported some really scary stuff but had a normal life otherwise." Penny ran a thumb over the edge of the stack of paper.

"Or he could have seen some horrible things and did his best to keep it separate from his everyday life. Kept it boring on purpose, to make up for all the scary stuff he had to report for his work."

Mabel carried two plates of steaming Taco Shepherd's Pie to the table. Penny was starving and ate hers quickly, not caring that the corn chip topping was soggy. She was eager to start reading Toby's manuscript.

TWENTY SIX

Phin staggered under the weight of Dee's old television. There wasn't enough room for everyone to fit in the small den where Lydia spent much of her time. The back yard deck had been cleared of clutter, and Phin had moved the barbecue and several large planters onto the grass to make room for chairs.

"Are you sure a card table is strong enough to hold this thing? It's got to weigh at least sixty pounds," he managed between gasps.

"Don't worry about the table," Mabel said, touching his elbow to guide his movements. "Just get the TV on it in one piece."

"It would have been just fine on the ground." He grunted as he set it down on the table, which groaned but held the weight.

"We've got a lot of people coming out to watch this. Might as well set it all up nice for them. Dee made sandwiches and Tammy said she'd bring chips and dip. She even promised to leave her dogs home for a change. She wants to be able to say she was here with us for our show."

Roland Tyrrell's Culture Splash was due in less than half an hour. Roland's assistant had called Voodoo Café two days ago announcing the date and time of the special segment of his show. Mabel had wanted to have a party at the café, claiming it would be good for business. She'd suggested they rent two large-screen TVs and advertise it as a sort of anniversary celebration. It would be like another grand opening.

Dee and Phin had argued against it, both certain it would be nothing short of a disaster if Roland made them out to be ridiculous. It would only give the café a bad reputation and they'd lose business instead. Mabel had scoffed at them and tried to finagle Penny's vote but found that she was the only one who was enthusiastic about the upcoming TV show.

Phin wished he didn't have to be here for the program but had promised Dee he'd at least help out with the television. He could have come up with several reasons to be absent but she'd said please and had smiled. He'd been powerless to refuse, but he wasn't looking forward to seeing himself portrayed as some kind of freakish sideshow. He could only hope Roland would keep it short.

"I was thinking it might be easier for Mom if we brought her chair out," Dee said to him as she came outside. "She's going to be confused with all these people showing up. If we have her sitting in her usual chair it might help."

"Wouldn't it be easier on her if we left her in the den where everything is familiar?"

"Not if we've removed her entertainment. That's the only thing that keeps her in the room, otherwise she'll wander." Dee plugged the TV into the extension cord that stretched from a socket indoors and turned it on, standing back to check the angle. "She'll come hunting for it as soon as she hears it."

"How many people are you expecting?" Phin asked as Mabel waved from the doorway and pointed to a jumble of mis-matched chairs she'd borrowed from their neighbours.

Dee fanned her face in the sunshine. "I hope not too many, but Mabel is kind of vague about how many invites she put out there."

"All of our friends are coming," Mabel piped up, gesturing to Phin for help. He set the chairs in two semi-circles in front of the television.

"Mabel, we have a lot of friends," Dee said. "This deck isn't big enough to hold the whole town."

"I mean real friends. I didn't invite Ruth or that Dr Leonard, and the grocery store crew aren't any friends of mine. I asked Josie to come but told her she had to leave the kids home. I did invite Fritz but he's mad at us again, no surprise there."

There was a knock at the front door and Mabel hurried away to answer. Dee and Phin exchanged a look.

"If we're going to get Lydia's chair out here, it better be now. The show's due in twenty minutes."

"On second thought," Dee said, "I can probably put Mom in one of these chairs for the short while we'll be out here. By the time she starts getting fidgety it'll be over and I can just get her back to her usual spot."

"My lower back can never thank you enough for that kindness," Phin said gravely, and then smiled widely when Dee giggled. He loved to hear her laugh, something she didn't do hardly enough.

Her laugh was so brief it might never have happened. Dee looked away and reddened, her hands fumbling with the TV remote. She flipped through several channels until she found the one she was looking for. "I still need to bring out two of those smaller tables for the food," she mumbled and went inside.

He watched a commercial about laundry soap without really seeing it, wondering how he could keep spooking her like that. She'd held his gaze so briefly. Had she read his need to be near her in that split second? He'd have to be careful about what he showed on his face.

Dee had avoided talking to him directly since he'd kissed her two weeks ago. He could still feel the soft pressure of her lips on his. Did she regret letting him get that close? He didn't know what to do except give her the space she needed. They'd all been in shock over Toby's suicide but it wouldn't help to have Phin panting after her like a lovesick teenage boy.

Voices drifted out from the house and rose in volume as a group of women poured out the door, giggling and exclaiming at the set-up in the yard.

"This is perfect! Just like a movie premiere."

"Here, let me help you set up that table and we'll get all the food in one place."

"I hope I brought enough for everyone."

"How is poor Lydia?"

"We should have brought champagne."

"Oh, Phineas darling, come sit with us. We'll all watch together."

Had no men been invited? Penny appeared at the doorway with Jeff in tow and Phin sighed in relief. He waved at her and she pulled Jeff over to two chairs at the end of a row. She whispered in his ear and left him to hold her seat.

"There's at least fifteen people here already," she said, as she approached Phin.

"You know Mabel. She's determined to make a show of this no matter how bad it is."

"Do you think it's going to be a bomb?"

"That guy will make us out to be a joke." Phin turned away from the others. "Have you finished reading Toby's manuscript yet?"

"Yeah, but I can't tell you about it."

"Why not?"

"His letter said I had to give it to the publisher without showing it to anyone. It's bad enough I read it."

"I'm sure he knew you would and didn't care. Besides, he's dead. It doesn't matter anymore what he wanted. We could all read it and then you could give it to the publisher. Have you even called him yet?"

"It's a she, and no I haven't called. I just wanted to read what he'd written before handing it over." She jammed her hands into her pockets. "It's a sad story but really cool at the same time, and everyone's just going to have to wait."

"I get it," Phin said, remembering how compelling Toby's letter to him had been. He looked over at Dee, who sat next to her mother. Lydia was beaming at everyone and seemed delighted to have all these people around her. Dee had warned that in Lydia's mind they might all be eight years old and celebrating someone's birthday.

Phin headed for the other end of the row, walking in the grass to avoid the jumble of chairs. He smiled and returned greetings as he passed. He'd become used to his reluctant role in their small community, but this was on a whole new level. Broadcasted from Vancouver, the show would reach far and wide. Phin hoped the warm day would keep most folks outdoors and away from their televisions. He leaned against the fence next to where Dee sat holding Lydia's tea.

"I'll bet this gets so popular that they'll send it to all the big networks," Mabel exclaimed, as if she'd been reading his thoughts and picked up on his distaste of exposure. "We've got something here that no one else has anywhere in the country. Anyone can offer hot springs, camping and hiking, or spa resorts. What we give people is a glimpse of their future and a whole new way to open up and let a little magic in."

"I don't know that I could handle that kind of notoriety," Dee said as she handed the remote control to Phin. "It should be on any minute now."

Phin turned up the volume just as the show began. An impeccably groomed woman gave a brief synopsis of the day's news, her perfect white teeth framed by impossibly red lips. Everyone hushed to hear and only the birds accompanied her voice.

"We here at K-BOY TV are dedicated to bringing our viewers the latest happenings. Roland Tyrrell scours the province looking for exciting events for his weekly spot." She glanced to her left and her eyes widened before facing the camera again. "Well, folks, Roland has outdone himself this time," she said with a smile.

The camera panned left to a red velvet curtain. It swayed as if it had just swung closed. A deep voice intoned: "Roland Tyrrell's

Culture Splash is proud to bring you Cricket Lake's Voodoo Mystery Tour."

White smoke poured across the floor, rolling and curling upward in front of the curtain, which slowly began to part. Red and yellow lights flickered behind the curtain, and the smoke glowed eerily as it seeped through the parting velvet.

A drum began to beat and was joined by another, and accented with rattles. The smoke dissipated to show a dark backlit figure in a long robe with head bowed. The man's arms slowly rose to shoulder height then suddenly dropped. The drums went silent.

The robed figure raised his head and spoke in a monotone.

"Clacking bones and pots of tea. Turn of card to fortune see."

The backlight dimmed as another came up from the ground by the figure's feet. It traveled up the length of a deep purple robe with shiny black stars stamped all over it.

"Séances by candlelight. Waters healing toxic blight."

Roland's face was revealed and the corners of his mouth twitched at the snort of muffled laughter from the cameraman. His eyes were heavily lined, he wore a frizzy black wig, and a scraggly beard had been pasted onto his chin. It was braided and strung with colorful beads.

"Oh come on!" Phin spluttered. He turned to Mabel, who clapped her hands in glee.

"Wow! He looks just like you."

"Are you responsible for this?"

"I might have given him a picture or two of you."

"You two be quiet," Dee said with a grin. "We're trying to hear the show."

Roland kept a solemn face as more lights on the set came up and brightened the backdrop to show enlarged Tarot cards pasted on the wall.

"I had my fortune told a couple of weeks ago," he said and waved a languid hand at the figures behind him. *"I was told I would have a*

successful career and find love where I least expected it." He pointed off to the side and raised his voice. "*Judy. What did you hear in your reading?*"

"*I'm supposed to find love too,*" a woman yelled from off-camera. The crew laughed and Roland finally smiled.

"*Marty was told he'd meet the girl of his dreams and that he'd finally remember where he'd put something he thought he'd lost. Larry is going to meet a girl too. Let's hope it's not the same one Marty is waiting for.*"

They cut to a clip of Mabel's interview.

"*Last summer we threw a magic crystal into our lake and it cleared up a toxic spill.*"

"*I heard your toxic spill was a hoax.*"

"*People will believe what they want to believe, in spite of the evidence.*"

Roland's face filled the screen again, the close-up showing how badly his wig fit and that the fake beard was coming unglued under the hot lights.

"*That was Mabel Berkeley, one of several psychics who live in the small town of Cricket Lake. Here's a picture of Phineas Marshal, their self-proclaimed witch doctor.*" The screen split in two and Roland's face was shown side by side with a photo of Phin wearing the same eye makeup, though his scraggly beard and hair were his own.

"I've seen enough," Phin said weakly and pointed the remote at the television. Mabel jumped up and snatched it from his hand before he could press any of the buttons.

"I haven't," she said with a grin. "He's just getting started. They did a lot of interviews that day. Didn't I look great?" She raised the remote and increased the volume.

"I knew he'd make us out to be ridiculous."

"Shush."

The screen changed to a scene of their lake at sunset.

"*Cricket Lake is a beautiful setting for a vacation, with cabins to rent and a lake for swimming and fishing. There's a modern café and bakery on the main drag, where you can sit on the patio and eat the most delicious cookies in the world, with a pot of hot tea to wash it all down.*" Shots of the bakery flashed past, showing shelves of bread and rolls, the arts and crafts corner, mounds of fresh cookies and the patio filled with smiling customers.

"And after you've finished that cup of tea Mabel will be happy to read your fortune in the leaves left at the bottom of the cup."

A shot of Mabel wearing her yellow turban and false eyelashes filled the screen. Everyone in Dee's yard burst out laughing, including Mabel.

"And that's Cricket Lake, folks." Roland pulled off the wig and winced as he tore the beard from his chin. *"They're kind of weird. The offbeat off the beaten path. Would I recommend it? You bet. A couple of hours' drive and well worth the trip. Just remember to bring your own mug if you want coffee for the road."* He pulled the robe over his head and balled it up with the wig and beard, then threw it off to the side.

"On a more serious note," he said while he ran his hand through his hair and straightened his shirt. *"There was another event in Cricket Lake at nearly the same time we were interviewing our new psychic friends."*

Penny gasped as Toby Greer's face filled the screen. He was much younger and thinner but she recognized the man who had entrusted her with his written legacy.

"Some of you may remember Tobias Greer as the journalist who, in the mid-eighties, offered himself up as a hostage in exchange for the release of two women and their three children." The photo shrunk into the top right corner of the screen and Roland faced the camera again. *"He was a hero who spent years alone in prison before the U.N. showed up and set him free."*

The screen filled with a collage of newspaper headlines:

"Hero Saves Women and Children"

"Tobias Greer Journalist of the Year"

"Four Years in Central American Prison"

Roland stared into the camera and frowned. *"We were shocked to hear that not only was Toby Greer visiting Cricket Lake at the same time as our film crew was there, but that he chose that time and place to end his life.*

"We now know that he was dying with only weeks to live and that he'd gone to the lake to finish his memoirs. I hear the manuscript is going to be published and I for one am looking forward to reading it."

Soft background music came up and the camera zoomed out, showing a jumble of photos of Cricket Lake on the wall behind Roland.

"Go for the great food. Go for a dubious but fun psychic experience. Go on a pilgrimage to see the place where a modern hero chose to spend his last days. Whatever reason you choose, go to Cricket Lake. You won't regret it."

Mabel clicked the remote and the television turned off. "Wow, that was amazing," she said with a grin. "Everyone is gonna want to come here now. We're famous!" She looked around but most of their friends were headed to the food table.

"Toby didn't think he was a hero," Penny said.

"Are you kidding? He saved those women and their kids," Phin said.

"Look, I'm supposed to keep the stuff in the book a secret until it gets published but I can't stand to be the only person who knows till then." She wiped her eyes on her sleeve and sniffed loudly. "All that footage of him surrendering back then and those soldiers letting the women and kids go was a sham. I mean, he did offer to trade places with them and the soldiers did let them go, but later he found out they'd arrested the women again."

Penny's lip trembled. "That's why it's so sad and he was sick and depressed his whole life afterwards. The soldiers made him watch while they beat those women to death and then told him all about how they'd sold the little kids off as slaves.

"They said the women had been sentenced to die because they'd left their husbands, and that he'd have been better off to write his stupid story and hope the United Nations came to their rescue in time. They'd have had a better chance to survive if he hadn't given himself up in trade. His captors laughed at him and reminded him of what he'd done every day until it nearly made him crazy.

"By the time he was rescued he was so ashamed and in shock that he couldn't tell the world about what he'd done.

Everyone thought he'd saved those women but all he'd done was buy himself years of torture."

"But at least he tried," Mabel said. "His actions made him a hero. No one else would have done that. How was he supposed to know he was being tricked?"

"All that torture was why he was dying. He had three kinds of cancer, stuff I can't even pronounce, because those soldiers thought it was funny to give him poisons that made him sick for months at a time." Penny turned to Jeff, who hugged her close while she sobbed on his shoulder.

Mabel touched Phin's arm and pointed to Lydia, who had fallen asleep in her chair. Phin picked up the frail woman, careful not to wake her. She was heavier than the television but considerably less awkward to carry. Phin cradled her to his chest and followed Mabel and Dee into the house.

TWENTY SEVEN

Phin spotted Dee, Mabel and Penny coming up the road, each clutching an umbrella against the pouring rain. He sighed and set down his cold coffee, put on a jacket and zipped it to his throat.

The rain had held off for two days, the leaden clouds and brisk winds threatening to drown out the busiest weekend of the summer. Phin had had to help out at the café when Dee dragged Penny into the kitchen to help her roll out pie crusts so they could keep up.

Phin had made countless pots of tea and carried them out to the patio on trays, only to return to the kitchen with a load of dirty dishes and orders for more. He couldn't believe Penny did this job every day with a smile.

Mabel was kept busy in her alcove, telling fortunes with tea leaves or Tarot cards. Every moment she had free was taken up with talking to curious tourists who had seen their television special on *Culture Splash*.

Dee worried about Mabel working too hard. Her aunt was exhausted at the end of each day and her voice was hoarse from so much talking, but Mabel couldn't be stopped. She was so excited by the attention their town was getting that she was driven to talk or sell or read fortunes for all comers.

Phin hooked a hammer into a belt loop and put several nails in his jacket pocket. He pulled on his boots and clomped down the steps just as the group arrived. He squinted in the pelting rain.

"Do we really need to do this now?"

"We agreed we'd put it up as soon as Jeff finished the engraving." Mabel turned to Penny, who was carrying the brass plaque against her chest. "He even drilled holes in the corners to make it easy to attach it to the wall of the cabin." She held out her hand and waggled her fingers. "Come on kiddo, give it up. My feet aren't getting any dryer out here."

Penny stuck her tongue out at Mabel and handed the plaque to Dee instead. It was shaped like an open book, its brass pages inscribed in wobbly calligraphy:

"This cabin is dedicated to Tobias Greer, a true Canadian hero."

Dee followed Phin onto the low deck of the last cabin in the row. She held the plaque against the front wall and turned her head away while Phin banged nails into the corners of the plaque, securing it to the wood. Mabel and Penny huddled together at the other end of the deck, sharing one umbrella.

"Shouldn't we say something?" Penny said softly.

"Why don't you tell Dee and Phin the rest of what Toby said in his letter to you?" Mabel put her arm around Penny's shoulder and gave her a squeeze. "Tell them what he wanted for his book."

Penny swallowed and her eyes filled with tears. "He said I reminded him of his wife, and not just because we shared the same name. She was about my age when she died having their baby. The baby was already dead when it was born. He went away, travelled the world, taking pictures and writing stories about people. It took his mind off her, for a little while at a time anyway." She took a shaky breath.

"I thought he hated kids," Dee said. "He complained about Josie's boys when they played on the beach and said they made too much noise."

"He said in the letter that they reminded him of the kids in the poor countries he'd been to who didn't have parents or toys but still played and just ran around and yelled and laughed."

"He sounds like he got maudlin in his old age."

"He wasn't so old, not even sixty yet. He just looked older because he was so sick." Penny ran her fingers over the words on the plaque and smiled sadly. "He said any money that's made from the sale of the book is to go to kids. He wants playgrounds built in as many places as possible, starting with Cricket Lake."

"The kids here don't need a playground as much as those kids who don't have anything," Mabel said.

Penny shook her head. "Nope they don't, but that's what he wrote. He'd been all over the world and said that Cricket Lake was the best hometown he'd ever had, so these kids should have a playground."

"At least it'll keep the tourists' kids from hanging around the café all the time," Mabel said. "Nothing worse than when they start going through all our displays, moving stuff around and playing with the wooden animals. We're not a petting zoo." Her eyebrows shot up. "Hey, I'm gonna make up a sign that says exactly that, put it up over the display."

"Sure, give everyone another reason to think we're weirdos." Phin jammed his hammer in his back pocket and walked a few feet away from the cabin to admire the shiny new plaque.

"You know," Mabel said musingly, "I kinda wish we had plaques for the other cabins. It would be good for business. I'll bet this one will be booked solid all year."

"Don't get any bright ideas," Dee said. "This was a tragedy. Do we really want to capitalize on that?"

"Death is good for business. I wonder if we'll be able to tell if Toby is haunting the cabin?"

"Mabel! That's creepy." Penny turned away and ran across Cricket Lake Road, and onto the beach.

"I'm not saying that they all have to be dedicated to dead people but we can at least think about it, right?" She yelled as she hurried to catch up with Penny, who giggled and put her hands over her ears.

Phin shook his wet hair out of his eyes and glanced at Dee. She'd been quiet for days and he'd been afraid to ask about it after glimpsing a stack of pamphlets in the café kitchen featuring various nursing homes in Vancouver. He knew she'd made several phone calls to prospective homes as well as to some of the larger bakeries in the city. Dee would never send Lydia into care without living near her.

"You know that everyone wants to help with Lydia," he began tentatively.

Dee looped her arm through his and drew closer as they walked. He shivered at her touch and wished he could find a way to keep her in Cricket Lake. He considered it the home he'd never had and couldn't bear to leave it, though he would follow her anywhere she chose to lead him. If she wanted him to, that is.

"What's happening to Mom scares me half to death. Part of me wants nothing more than to give her up to people who can take proper care of her and to visit once in a while. I'd be able to have a normal life." She squeezed his arm closer to her side. "But I'd have to live in the city, away from everyone else I love. And I'd be alone because she wouldn't be there when I got home from work."

"You could live here and go visit."

"Nope. Too much guilt." She smiled sadly.

"The café and the cabins make enough money combined to support us all and we'll all help to make sure Lydia is looked after."

"I could never ask you and Penny to shoulder that burden. Mabel and I are Mom's family and she's our responsibility."

Phin stopped and gripped her by the arms, shaking her gently. "You're my family. You're Penny's family. You and Mabel and Lydia took us in and made us part of your lives. Please don't leave." He pulled her into his arms abruptly, nearly lifting her off her feet.

Dee hugged him fiercely, then pulled back just enough so she could look into his eyes. Phin had come into town and turned her life upside down, collapsing illusions about her past and crashing open family secrets. He'd wormed his way into her heart and had brought love and chaos, never asking for more than she could bear to give back.

She leaned forward and pressed her lips to his, the first kiss since the one he'd surprised her with at the café. Their skin was wet and cold from the rain but the warmth of the kiss spread quickly and Phin pulled her against his chest.

They broke apart at a screech of laughter and turned to watch Mabel and Penny dragging logs and rocks onto the sand. It looked like they were already laying out the foundation for the playground.

Phin stood behind Dee, wrapped his arms around her and rested his chin on her head. She snuggled into his embrace and laughed as Mabel lost her grip on the log and fell onto the wet sand with a squeak.

"I suppose I might as well stay," she said. "Someone has to keep an eye on those two."

DELETED SCENES FROM:

TYE DYE VOODOO

&

VOODOO MYSTERY TOUR

1. The Great Nico

2. Ella's Attic

3. Crow's Nest Pie

4. Josie's Boys

5. Mabel's Sixty-Nine

   (In Three Acts)

6. Cat Lady

7. Cookbook Hijack

The Great Nico

The sun had set and the clouds drifting across the western sky had cycled through a spectacular rainbow. They'd since dispersed, leaving a pure deep indigo as a backdrop for the first stars.

Nico leaned against the railing and gazed down into the dark waters of the Atlantic. He had cancelled his return flight and bought passage on this ship after he'd left the meeting with the Consortium. He would have been home by now had he stuck to his plans, but his once-in-a-lifetime meeting had changed everything. The close confines of a plane would have been too dangerous.

He shivered in the rising wind and pulled his coat closed. Time to retire to his cabin and try to get some rest. He rubbed his hands together briskly and reached down for his satchel. It wasn't there. A young man stood a few feet away holding the bag and staring at it with open-mouthed wonder and fear.

Nico marched up to him and snatched it from his hands. "It appears you've picked up the wrong bag."

"Give that back," the man shouted, lunging for it. He grabbed the handle of the satchel and tugged, but Nico stepped back and clutched it tightly to his chest.

"What's the problem here?" A steward came running and stepped between the two men, causing the younger man to lose his grip.

"That old guy just stole my bag!" He tried to reach past the steward but Nico stayed out of his grasp.

"Is that true?" the steward turned to Nico.

"No. This satchel is mine. If you would like to check, the tag attached to the handle matches my identification."

"All right then, let's see your I.D." The steward pushed away the other man, who continued to protest and reach for the bag.

Nico reluctantly handed it to the steward and retrieved his wallet from the inside pocket of his coat. The wind whipped across the deck and he shivered as he dug through the wallet. He glanced at the steward, who seemed mesmerized by the satchel. The would-be-thief's hand was now touching the smooth leather, but he had not tried to take it again.

Nico cleared his throat and held out his passport for the steward to see. The man ignored him and Nico felt a fleeting moment of panic. What if he decided to confiscate the bag? "Sir?"

The steward looked at him with a dreamy expression and seemed confused, as if he'd forgotten why he was there.

"My identification," Nico said and shoved the passport under the man's nose. "Nicholas Minkley. As you can see, it clearly matches the name on the tag."

"Yes, right," the steward mumbled, his gaze still unfocused.

Nico reached for the bag and pried the steward's stiff fingers from the handle. He moved away quickly, heading for the far side of the ship. He could hear the steward talking to the young man, who was now apologizing profusely and saying that he had no idea what had come over him. Nico didn't need an apology. It was the third such incident since he'd boarded the ship yesterday.

He found a quiet spot and balanced the satchel on the railing, holding the strap tightly. All he had to do was open the box inside and tip it overboard. No one would notice. The crystal would be gone and so would the danger that the next thief would be more successful in taking it from him.

He closed his eyes and tried to convince himself that he was doing the right thing by disposing of it, that he was ridding the world of a dangerous artefact. He vaguely wondered if his thinking might be impaired by the crystal's proximity.

****

Two days ago:

Nico was thrilled at the invitation from the International Magicians' Consortium to attend their annual retreat. He had applied for membership several times but had been regularly refused admission because of his youth and lack of experience. It was an honour to be invited, despite last year's rejected application, but now he suspected he'd only been accepted because they were desperate. They were all so old, the youngest at least twice Nico's age.

The ceremony was solemn, though rushed, and more than one attendee was skeptical of Nico's suitability as a peer. Cedric, their leader, argued that Nico was a perfect candidate. There were also speeches, the last of which had laid out Nico's chief responsibility as a new member of the Consortium: to guard their most revered artefact.

A curtain was drawn back to reveal a padlocked iron box sitting on a pedestal inside a glass case. Everyone in the room cringed at the sight of the box and became quiet except for a very old man sitting in a wheelchair.

"It's here, isn't it?" he whispered, raising his nose in the air as a dog would at an enticing scent. He struggled to his feet and his attendant rushed to untangle the thin hose that ran from the old man's nose to the oxygen tank strapped to the back of the chair.

"Gordon, please sit down," Cedric said, gesturing to the attendant.

Gordon protested, pushing away his attendant's hands. "I may no longer be able to see the crystal, but I'm not blind to its power." A few uncertain steps and he faced the iron box. He reached out a hand and his mouth curled up briefly before he winced and his knees gave way. His attendant expertly steered the wheelchair underneath him and the old man fell into it with a grunt.

"You can't seriously consider sending it away," Gordon said, weakly.

"We've discussed this ad nauseum." Cedric briefly glanced at Nico before continuing. "It's time we injected some new blood into this Consortium. We haven't allowed any new members for nearly a decade and, frankly, we're no longer equipped to handle this level of guardianship." He turned back to Nico. "As you can see, young man, we're all getting on in years."

Gordon protested and his attendant tried to quiet him. "I will not be shushed," he said peevishly. "We agreed a long time ago that it should never leave our hands."

"That was before we knew the downside to its power."

"Downsides are for wimps," Gordon said, his voice rising. "We have a responsibility to protect others from this danger."

"That's why we're recruiting a new member. Nico is more than qualified to guard the crystal on our behalf."

"But you're sending it halfway across the planet. The aliens won't like that."

Cedric glanced at Nico again as the rest of the group laughed nervously. "Pay no attention to Gordon. He's got some wild ideas about the crystal's origin, but you can be sure that he's alone in this delusion."

Nico looked at the other men in the room but none would make eye contact. "Aliens?"

"Yes!" Gordon shouted. His attendant whispered in his ear and Gordon slapped him. "Get away. I can't believe you all still won't accept the truth. The boy needs to know that the crystal is a homing beacon and is collecting human energy to power its signal to alert the aliens." He leaned toward Nico and lowered his voice.

"It's a potent alien mind-fuck that men can't resist," he said in a rush. His blind eyes seemed to bore into Nico. "It steals a bit of your life force each time you commune with it but leaves you with psychic residue that is addictive. It's a trap that is setting us up for an alien invasion!"

Cedric signalled to Gordon's attendant and the man turned the wheelchair toward the exit. "Gordon suffers from dementia and has been having hallucinations and delusions," he said to Nico.

Gordon railed as he was wheeled away. "Throw it in the ocean. Water muffles the signal. It's the only thing that will save you!" His last words came out in a wheezy whimper and then he was gone.

None of the others spoke during Gordon's outburst but they all fidgeted nervously, looking longingly at the box under the glass. Eight old men, all with terrified expressions on their weathered faces. Nico also stared at the box, wondering what was inside that could frighten such experienced men.

He tried to politely refuse but they implied that to refuse this task would effectively bar him from their group forever. How could he turn down the great honour that he'd been offered? The greatest magicians and illusionists in the world had not only invited him to join their ranks but had made him a guardian of one of their most revered treasures.

In a big hurry to send him on his way, they thanked him profusely as they pushed him out the door. Just before it slammed shut, Cedric put a shaking hand on the satchel they'd given Nico.

"Pay no mind to Gordon's rant," he whispered, his gnarled fingers grasping the bag's heavy leather.

"Where's this thing *really* from?" Nico pleaded.

"If anyone has ever known its origins, it's Gordon, and you've seen what condition his mind is in. The general story is that he found the crystal in a box of fake gems. He told me the gems came from a theatre auction in Paris. He told Zachary he bought them from a Greek gypsy at a midnight market. Others got the Malaysian mail-order story, and you've heard the alien angle." Cedric reluctantly released his grip on the satchel.

"All I know is that we've been taking turns being the crystal's keeper for far too long. We are old men, and we have grown weak. It is our fervent desire that it be removed from our reach and not one will fault you if it ends up lost in the deepest part of the Atlantic."

****

The ship rolled under Nico's feet and his fingers tightened reflexively on the satchel. Could he just toss it overboard? It would be very easy to drop the crystal over the side of the boat and into the water. No one would ever find it again.

He hadn't slept last night, trying to convince himself that Gordon had indeed been demented and that he should ignore his rant about alien homing beacons. He'd lain in the narrow bunk wondering if he'd sold his soul to the devil. He wasn't a religious man and had rarely accompanied Ella to church on Sundays. He didn't believe in a higher being, but he did believe in evil.

Nico opened the satchel and lifted out the wooden box. It should have been nearly as cold as the chill air that was making him shiver, but the wood was almost too warm to touch. Could the crystal be radioactive? Gordon had been the crystal's guardian longer than anyone else. Radiation poisoning could have rotted his brain.

Nico unlocked and opened the box. A white-green light flared and he gasped in shock. His pulse hammered in his throat and he slammed the lid shut before anyone else could see it. In the few seconds that he'd beheld the brilliance his mind had filled with images of his life and career thus far, and of promised events that had not yet happened: visions of huge audiences enthralled by his impossible illusions, and posters boasting of The Great Nico and his amazing feats of magic.

His heart raced and he stared down at the surging waters of the Atlantic until his eyes had adjusted to the darkness again.

He now understood that those old men weren't part of the Consortium because they were great magicians, but that their

148

powers and successes had been a side effect of that beautiful light. Had Gordon recruited them all the same way that Nico had been selected?

He forced his limbs to move, slipping the box back into the satchel with trembling hands. How could he abandon such a precious jewel? He knew he was being unreasonable and fear rose again as he realized it didn't matter whether or not Gordon had been telling the truth.

The crystal held a great power. Nico could feel it coursing wildly through his body and mind, and he didn't care where it came from, only that he had to protect it at all cost. The cold wind whipped through his hair and he hugged the satchel tightly to his chest as he returned to his cabin to wait out the rest of the voyage, alone with his prize.

Ella's Attic

The wooden slats creaked and groaned as Phineas gingerly eased his weight onto the old steamer trunk. The late afternoon light painted the room in shades of fire, and every crate and armoire cast an elongated shadow, creating a smudged cityscape that slowly edged sideways across the floor.

Phin sipped his cold take-out coffee as he sat and watched Penny roam the attic. She poked her head into a square opening next to the chimney and pulled it out again quickly. She slid a panel into place to cover the hole, which left it barely discernible from the rest of the wall.

Penny had been nervous about coming into Ella's house. She'd twitched at every unexpected sound as they packed up the place. She had only reluctantly climbed the ladder into the attic after Phin had gone up and left her alone downstairs.

"I wonder if Eric had been selling Ella's valuables," Phin said.

"That weasel probably sold everything he could get his hands on."

"At least it makes it easier for us to know what's worth keeping."

"How about this?" Penny asked. She pulled a fur coat from a box and slipped her arms into the sleeves. She slapped the front of the coat and coughed as great billows of dust rose up.

Phin snorted laughter. "I was hoping more for something my great-uncle might have left about the crystal." He gestured to the boxes they'd stacked near the trap door in the floor. "It's all junk. Busted top hats and mouldy black capes. Not a single letter or diary. I mean, who keeps boxes of musty fake flower bouquets and broken bird cages?"

"If there was anything in this house about that stupid crystal, Eric would have found it. The guy was obsessed." Penny shivered and took off the fur, tossing it into a box and creating another dust cloud.

"If Eric had found anything he wouldn't have sent you to Cricket Lake."

"At least he missed Ella's safe or you'd never have gotten this house."

It was Phin's turn to shiver, and he stood abruptly. It was the second time in only a year that a woman had died violently and left Phin as heir to all her worldly possessions. The last thing he'd wanted was another house filled with an old woman's mementos, faded furniture covered in doilies, and far more towels than any one person could ever use.

A realtor had come around to appraise it. Phin said to sell it fast, and that he wasn't interested in haggling over price. He'd empty it and have a cleaning service prep it for showing within a week. The realtor had sent a local charity and their large truck. They'd filled it with all the furniture, countless boxes of dishes, and bags of clothing and linens.

Phin and Penny had boxed up the dozens of framed photos covering the walls, along with several albums of family photos they'd found on a shelf in Ella's bedroom closet. Phin hoped Mabel might recognize some of the faces and help him piece together his past.

"Not much left here, just this trunk and those two boxes."
He opened the trunk, which was half-filled with old newspapers
and show posters that were yellowed and crumbling at the edges.
They all featured the Great Nico. The corner of Phin's mouth
twitched upward. He'd recently discovered an interesting family
he'd never known he had, and they were all dead. Phin put the
posters aside to take home.

The rest of the trunk held a pile of old running shoes and a
stack of t-shirts. He shook out one of the shirts. The front was
covered in rows of faint symbols.

"These look like some kind of Viking runes," he called to
Penny.

She whirled to face him and her mouth dropped open at the sight
of the shirt. Her cheeks flushed a bright pink and she snatched it out of
his hands and escaped down the ladder to the main floor.

Phin's eyebrows rose and he shrugged. He reached into the trunk
for the rest of the stack. Mabel said to keep an eye out for souvenir t-
shirts. He wondered how she'd known they'd be here.

Crow's Nest Pie

Mabel carefully set a second pie on the table. She shuffled the other entries around to make them all fit, careful to keep the accompanying labels with the correct pies.

She was glad they'd decided to hold the recipe contest outdoors this year. It was such a beautiful day it would be impossible to entice folks indoors. People browsed the four display tables set out under two open-sided tents, admiring and judging the entries in this year's categories: pies and gelatin.

Mabel had submitted two entries in each category.

"All that gelatin is going to melt in this heat," Penny said, ducking in under the tent awning. She handed Mabel a glass of lemonade. Ice clinked in the cold drink and the outside of the glass was beaded with condensation.

"I sure hope not, kiddo, though both mine are based on hot foods so that might not be a bad thing." She took a long sip of lemonade and sighed in pleasure.

"Why you think anyone would ever eat onion soup jello is beyond me." Penny made a face. "It smells disgusting."

"You won't know until you've tried it," Mabel countered. "Remember the bacon and egg lasagna? You had no issues with that combo."

A chorus of high-pitched barking erupted at the other end of the park. Tammy had tied her four small dogs to a tree and was heading toward the pie tent. The dogs yapped and strained at the ends of their leashes to follow their mistress.

"So what have you come up with this year?" Tammy called out as she approached.

"These two are mine," Mabel answered, proudly pointing out entries whose tented cards read *Crow's Nest Pie* and *MagPie*.

Tammy examined *Crow's Nest Pie* with a skeptical frown. The pan bristled with fried chow mein noodles surrounding four hard-boiled eggs dyed blue-green and speckled with black. "How's this a pie?" she asked, snapping off a piece of crunchy noodle.

"There's a crust so it's a pie. You just have to peel the eggs before you eat it." Mabel stroked the tip of one egg and smiled fondly at her creation.

Tammy waved a hand dismissively and moved on to *MagPie*. It looked like a normal pie, but the top crust didn't quite fit, as if it had been baked separately.

"*MagPie*? Really, Mabel. Tell me you didn't actually go bird hunting."

"This one's a pun," Mabel said with a grin. "Magpies love shiny things so I've filled it with little toys and trinkets."

"Kind of like a piñata only you don't hit it with a stick," Penny added helpfully.

"But you have to be able to eat it," Tammy exclaimed. "You can't call it pie if it isn't edible!"

"I put candy in it too. Besides, nothing in the rules said it had to be edible," Mabel said, deliberately rolling her eyes to a pie sitting on the far corner of the table. It had a dark crumbly top over what looked like a normal bottom crust.

"This pie is completely edible." Tammy straightened out the card that read *Canine Delight*.

Penny sniffed it delicately. "Ew, it stinks."

"That's because it's canned dog food," Mabel said with a grin.

"Speaking of inedible…" Penny backed away from the pie.

"I only feed my babies the best," Tammy said as she moved the card another fraction. "This recipe is so high-grade it could pass inspection for human consumption."

"And what about those bits on top?"

"That's an expensive daily supplement that also cleans their teeth."

"Looks like rabbit turds," Penny muttered as she took Mabel's empty lemonade glass and slipped out of the tent. Her break was nearly over and she was due back at the café in five minutes. She hurried past the tree where Tammy's four dogs had hopelessly tangled their leashes and were sitting quietly, uneasily eyeing the only other dog in the park, a huge bull mastiff bearing straight for them. It outweighed young Todd, who held the leash tightly as he was practically dragged across the grass.

The dog ignored the boy's shouts in its eagerness to play with the four bundles of quivering fur but paused as it reached Penny, wagging its tail. She scratched velvety ears and smiled at Todd, who was bent over and gasping. She felt the dog tense as it raised its nose in the air, sniffing and turning in a circle.

Todd cried out "No, Maxie!" and fell on his face, losing the leash as the dog lunged away.

Tammy's dogs barked shrilly as Maxie sped past them with Penny and Todd in hot pursuit. Penny tried vainly to step on Maxie's leash, but the dog had a head start and was widening the gap between them as he headed for the pie tent.

"Incoming!" she shouted, to warn Mabel and Tammy, who turned at her voice in time to dive out of the way. Maxie snatched *Canine Delight* off the corner of the table and ran off with his prize clamped firmly in his jaws. The crowd cheered and clapped as Tammy raced after the dog, screeching in fury.

"We should give her the prize for most entertaining pie," Penny said, gasping for breath.

Mabel grinned and moved the other pies around to fill the empty corner. "At least she proved it was edible."

Josie's Boys

Phin watched bemusedly as the two boys emptied the contents of their bulging pockets onto the scarred wooden table. He sorted through the mess, discarding rocks, sticks and crumbly leaves. Eight-year-old Todd had a very broad understanding of what Phin needed and he pocketed anything that looked interesting. The resulting leftovers were a motley assemblage of broken rib bones and vertebrae from local deer or raccoons. He wondered where they managed to uncover so many more bones than he'd been able to find in the local woods.

Phin picked up a few of the smaller pieces and nodded his satisfaction, earning him a pair of nearly identical grins. He used very few of the bones the boys brought, but had learned that choosing only the specific pieces he wanted resulted in the boys demanding individual payment for each bone. It was cheaper to pay for the entire haul and dispose of the remains later.

"What's in the bundle?" he asked.

Charlie grinned and carefully set the bundle he'd been cradling against his chest on the table. Where Todd was a generous boy and picked up anything in the woods he thought Phin might like, his brother was clearly out to make some cash.

"This is the best part," Charlie said excitedly. He unrolled the stained towel, exposing a pile of bleached bones and a folded sheet of paper. He flattened the paper and quickly arranged the bones to match the diagram on the page. When he was satisfied he slid the paper over to Phin. "The whole skeleton is there," he said. "There's not a single bone missing."

"What was it?"

"It's Rupert, my pet rabbit. He died a long time ago."

"Why do you still have Rupert's skeleton and how is it so clean?"

"I dug him up last week," he said proudly. "I read on the Internet how to boil it first to get the last bits of flesh off and then bleach the bones so they won't look bloodstained."

"It was really stinky," Todd said solemnly.

Phin opened his mouth but snapped it shut when he realized he had no idea how to respond to that. Would Josie have allowed her son to boil and then bleach a skeleton he had dug out of the ground? Did she even know he'd done it? He hoped the boy had at least cleaned the pot when he'd finished his dubious rabbit stew.

"I have a bunny, too," Todd chimed in. "His name was Eddie and you can have him, too, if you want."

His brother pushed him aside roughly. "Don't be dumb. I told you he doesn't want your stupid dead rabbit. Eddie only died last month. He's not even a real skeleton yet."

Phin tried not to smile, grateful to Charlie for preventing his brother from digging up what was probably a juicily decomposing rabbit by now. He felt a little sorry for Todd, whose eyes were glistening with tears, though he couldn't tell whether from the loss of his pet rabbit or the rebuke.

He eyed the pile on the table, mentally tallying up what was useful and how much he should offer. "I'll give you two bucks for the lot," he said with a straight face, knowing that they would protest whatever he offered. He wasn't disappointed.

"You gotta be kidding!" Todd exclaimed, stamping around the yard and punching the air. It was his standard reaction and never varied.

"Not enough," Charlie said flatly and crossed his arms.

"It's mostly broken bits of bones and rocks," Phin said. "Take it or leave it."

"The rabbit alone is worth at least ten bucks." The boy picked up the rabbit skull and thrust it at Phin, who reached out to take it from him.

"Most of that skeleton is too fragile to be of…" he faltered as his fingers gripped the skull, and his breath caught in his throat. An intense vibration emanated from the tiny bone. The tremor ran up his arm and slammed into his chest and belly. His heart rate spiked and he felt a sudden urge to run like hell for the nearest hole, coupled with a hunger so all-encompassing he barely stopped himself from stuffing the rabbit skull into his mouth.

He dropped the skull on the table and earned a scowl from Charlie, who gently lined it up with the rest of the skeleton.

"Ten for the rabbit and *five* for the rest," the boy insisted.

Phin took a shuddering breath. Still unable to speak, he dug into his pocket and pulled out a few wrinkled bills. He thrust a ten and a five at Charlie, who snatched the money and ran off with Todd in pursuit, yelling for his share.

Phin reached a trembling hand toward the rabbit skull and felt such a sudden gut-wrenching terror again that he nearly wet himself. He pulled his hand back and the terror eased. Mostly. This skull was smaller than his fox skull but packed a huge punch. Where the fox had been crushed by a falling woodpile and had not seen death coming, the rabbit had likely been killed by a half-starved predator, judging by the desperate hunger mixed in with the rabbit's fear.

He nearly leapt out of his skin when a voice called to him from the other side of the closest cabin.

"That little con artist played you like a badly-tuned violin," Toby drawled.

Phin concentrated on breathing slowly so that his heart might take the hint and stop jackhammering his ribcage.

"Most of this is crap – I heard you say so – and yet you accepted his ridiculous counteroffer." Toby picked up the tiny rabbit skull and Phin lurched to his feet, ready to slap it away from his hand, but his friend was examining the skull closely and without any apparent side effects.

"He really did do a very good job of cleaning these bones," Toby said, glancing toward the road where the boys had disappeared. "Con artist might be too mild a term for that boy."

Mabel's Sixty-Nine
(In Three Acts)

Act One

Penny carried the cake through from the kitchen to the living room, where Dee had decorated for Mabel's birthday party. "Good thing we went for numeral candles or I might set something on fire walking through the house," she joked as she set the cake on the low coffee table.

"It looks fantastic!" Mabel ran a finger through a blue ribbon of frosting and plopped it in her mouth. "Mm." She closed her eyes in appreciation.

"It's my first cake," Penny said with a grin. "I mean, I just did the decorating. Dee baked it."

Dee handed Mabel a knife. "Just a small slice for me and give Mom a corner piece so she's got lots of frosting."

"That's one thing Lydie and I always had fights over when we were kids. Whose piece of cake had the most frosting on it was a huge matter of concern." Mabel set a slice of cake on the tray in her sister's lap. She cut a bite with a fork and brought it close to Lydia's mouth. "Eat your cake, Lydie," she whispered. Lydia's head turned toward Mabel and her eyes widened at the sight of the cake. She took the fork from Mabel's hand and fed herself.

Mabel watched her sister eat birthday cake for a few moments, knowing that when the plate was empty the fork would fall from Lydia's hand and her gaze would return to the window to stare emptily at the world outside.

"Mabel, sit over there next to Phin and I'll bring your cake and tea." Penny carried a tray to Mabel, who balanced it on her lap and waited for the others to settle. She peered into her cup, at the tea leaves crowded together at the bottom, and wondered what they'd have to say once she'd drunk the brew.

"A toast to the birthday girl," Phin said, draining his tea in one long slurp.

Penny tapped her fork against the edge of her plate. "Speech! Come on, Mabel. The birthday girl should give a speech."

Mabel set aside her tray and stood up. "I'd like to start this speech with a joke." She plucked the two candles from the cake and held up the wax six and nine. "What's sixty-nine and sixty-nine?" She looked at each puzzled face in turn before grinning and yelling gleefully: "Dinner for four!"

"I don't get it," Penny said, giggling nervously and glancing at Dee, who was staring open-mouthed at her aunt.

"Dirty jokes? Really, Mabel," Dee finally managed to say. She turned to Phin, who sat with one hand covering his face, shoulders shaking with laughter. "Don't encourage her," she said, slapping Phin's knee.

"Come on, Chickadee. It's a once in a lifetime opportunity to take advantage of my age. I'll never get to do it again."

"What? Tell a dirty joke at a birthday party?"

"Even better," Mabel said, rubbing her hands together. "I've been saving up for years waiting for this day."

"Saving up for what?" Phin asked, wiping tears of laughter from his eyes.

"I've always had this dream of telling sixty-nine jokes about sixty-nine while I was sixty-nine."

"Why would you want to do that? It's ridiculous," Dee protested.

Phin snickered again and held up a finger for attention. "Sorry to point out the flaw in your plan, but you just turned sixty-nine. That means you're in your seventieth year. Shouldn't you have done this last year?"

Mabel gave him a withering look. "I come up with a fun plan and you're fixated on my age. Are you calling me old?"

"Just pointing out the obvious."

She ignored him. "How about another joke?" She smiled and continued despite several head shakes. "What's the square root of sixty-nine?" Mabel bounced on the balls of her feet as she paused long enough to give them time to answer. "Ate something!"

"That isn't even a real joke," Penny said. She picked up her plate and cup and gestured for Phin to pass his.

"No one appreciates sexy math humour."

Mabel looked at Phin. He rolled his eyes.

"It's funnier if you see it written down," she said glumly.

Act Two

Mabel tapped the tarot cards together and set the deck aside. She took the twenty dollar bill the woman handed her across the small table with a smile of thanks.

"I hope the cards answered your question," she said to Charlotte, who nodded.

"What you said about patience and kindness is a good reminder, especially in this case. We're heading to my in-laws' cottage north of here first thing in the morning and I'll need to be patient with Joe's mother."

"Where are you staying tonight?"

"We've got a room at that place by the highway."

Mabel leaned forward conspiratorially. "There's not much to do after-hours around here so I've got a couple of jokes you can tell your husband later." She winked. "What do you call oral sex between boomers? Sixty-something."

Before Charlotte could react, Mabel launched into another. "What is six point nine? Sixty-nine interrupted by a period! Love that one," she said, chuckling. She stood and Charlotte lurched to her feet a moment later.

"I don't know about you," Mabel said, as she grasped the edge of the curtain that shielded the alcove from Voodoo Café, "but it's been so long since I've had a period, you'd think I'd get laid more often."

She yanked the curtain aside and nearly bumped into Dee, whose face was flushed with stormy anger. Mabel peered over her niece's shoulder. A dozen faces stared at her, half of them children.

"Oh."

Act Three

Phin watched Mabel, who sat across the table from him. She'd knocked on his door half an hour ago and demanded a reading. He was suspicious, as it was three days since her last one and several days until the new moon. She was shuffling tarot cards but her small hands couldn't manage the oversized deck and several cards slipped to the table.

"Spit it out," he demanded, prying the deck from her fingers and scooping up the stray cards.

"You know my birthday is in two days," she began, and waited for Phin to nod before continuing. "I'm coming up a little short on joke-telling."

Phin closed his eyes and set the cards on the table. He'd hoped that Mabel would eventually get tired of the negative reaction she got from most of her special jokes. Most of them had been pretty lame but had managed to sound either excruciatingly embarrassing or dirtier than usual only because of who was telling them.

"Fine, tell me a joke. One joke." He sat back and folded his arms, bracing himself for the inevitable uncomfortable pause at the end of the punch line.

"So, why can't Miss Piggy count to seventy?" She paused and raised her eyebrows, grinning.

Phin sighed and pinched the bridge of his nose. He knew she would wait him out. He'd tested her more than once and they'd had one standoff that lasted two hours, where Mabel simply repeated the question every ten minutes until Dee stepped in and insisted she tell the punch line. Dee had then set some ground rules, one being that the joke had to be acknowledged so Mabel could deliver her punch line and let everyone get on with their day. "Gee, I don't know. Why can't Miss Piggy count to seventy?"

"Because every time she gets to sixty-nine she has a frog in her throat!"

Phin watched Mabel giggle with glee and tried to resist the tug at the corner of his mouth.

Mabel noticed. "How about another one?"

He held up a hand. "No. That's me done. I've done my duty. Find someone else to torture."

"What about the other day when you hung up on me? I didn't get to finish telling that one. I should get a do-over." She launched into the joke, talking rapidly. "What's a seventy-one? A sixty-nine with two fingers up…"

"Stop right there!" Phin said, slapping a hand on the table and making her jump. "There's a limit, and that's so far over the top I'm willing to throw you out if you finish that sentence. You've started that one twice now. I'm calling it done."

Mabel pouted and crossed her arms over her skinny chest. "No fair. It shouldn't count unless I get to finish it. Besides, I don't have a spare."

"I'm sure you've got a few left to tell."

"I've told sixty-two jokes, sixty-three if you count that last one. That makes six left to tell." She tilted her head and smiled. "Please?"

"Not a chance."

Mabel frowned. "I'm never going to make my deadline. Last week Dee said no more for her or Lydia – who doesn't count, by the way, because she's not really listening – and I've been banned from telling jokes in most of the stores in town."

"You should have thought of that when you came up with your scheme."

"Not fair," she complained again. "I've supported all your schemes."

"That's because you're the one who usually comes up with them. I'm always just dragged along for the ride."

"I could blackmail you."

"You've got nothing."

"Fine, you're forcing me to throw down my last card."

"What are you talking about?" Phin eyed her warily.

"Well, you know that Riva and I were once lovers," she began, and then nodded as Phin's expression belied his dismay at the unexpected topic. "That's right, dear, I'm throwing down the Step-Mom card."

"You can't be serious," Phin spluttered. "I wasn't even born yet when you…when she…er…"

"Oh you were around. Would you like to hear about how we met? Or about our first date?"

"No thanks." He glared at her through slitted eyes for a moment. "Here's the deal. I'll take a third of your jokes off your hands. That's two of the six."

"Not good enough, Son." Mabel grinned at his sour expression. "The fewer jokes you take, the more stories you get about me and your dear old Mom."

"This isn't a negotiation."

"I beg to differ." She regarded him blandly. "You get the three dirtiest jokes. I can probably fob off the milder ones somewhere else."

Phin rolled his eyes to the ceiling, thinking furiously. This always happened with Mabel. If he let her set the terms, she'd escalate them the next time this happened. "All right. Here's my final offer: you tell me the three mildest jokes and mail me the other three."

"You have to promise to read them before my birthday or it won't count."

"You'll have to trust that I will."

"I'll need to hit the post office before it closes so they'll get to you in time." She rubbed her hands together briskly. "Let's get started."

"You can wait another few minutes," Phin said as he got up from the table. "I'm going to need a fresh pot of coffee."

Cat Lady

Penny opened her eyes to pitch darkness. She couldn't move and had no idea where she was. She'd had a nightmare again about the time she'd woken up half-frozen, two winters ago, in the grimy recessed doorway of a store on Hastings Street with crazy Dumpster Man curled around her body, snoring his fetid breath in her face.

Her legs twitched and she almost cried out in relief that they still worked. But what was wrong with her arms? Was she tied up? Maybe she'd fallen asleep on a park bench again and had been picked up by the police. No. They always just woke her up, poking at her with their clubs and a "move along, kid."

She let slip a whimper of fear and was answered by a familiar meow.

"Castor?" she whispered.

Another meow, to her right, followed by a rumbling purr. Castor's brother Pollux, who never meowed, purred in tandem on her other side.

Penny sighed in relief. She was lying in her own bed, safe in the house she'd lived in since Phineas had moved out and insisted she stay. She'd tried to protest when he'd handed her the keys. She'd even offered to give him rent, but he'd said the house was paid for and she only had to deal with the taxes and utilities.

She had also tried to pretend she was annoyed at having to care for the several cats that came with the house, but had been so grateful for their furry company she hadn't been able to pull it off.

She tried to wiggle but her arms were pinned firmly at her side under the covers. Castor and Pollux snugged themselves more securely against her, lying on her hands and effectively clamping her to the bed. She laughed at her predicament and closed her eyes to enjoy the warm fuzzy company.

Penny wondered why so many people made fun of women who lived with multiple cats. Cat ladies probably got more love and attention than most people. Being a cat lady isn't so bad, she thought with a smile.

The bed creaked and Penny opened her eyes again. She recognized Orion's fluffy shape at the foot of the bed. His sleek black fur stood out against the faded quilt.

"Come here, kitty," Penny murmured, and tensed her muscles as Orion delicately stepped onto her stomach. He felt like a bowling ball stomping around her gut on four pointy chopsticks until he found his favourite spot and settled his belly against hers with a purr of contentment.

She sighed and relaxed, squinting at Orion in the early morning gloom. There was something wrong with his face – a gray lump against his snout. Then it fell away and landed on the blanket. She only had time to register what it was before it rolled under her chin, out of her line of sight. Dark wet strings dripped from Orion's fangs, and he wiped a paw over his snout to clean it.

Mouse! Penny tensed again but couldn't do anything more than waggle her feet and head. She glanced at Castor and Pollux. Their ears were twisted tightly backwards to keep tabs on Orion. They looked annoyed and she was surprised they hadn't left the bed. The twins didn't like to share space with Orion if they could help it. They'd had her attention first and now he had trumped them with his offering.

Phin had warned her about letting the cats have access to the bedroom and had suggested she keep the door shut at all times. She thought he'd meant it would keep their fur from getting into her clothing and on the bed. He'd neglected to mention hunter-cat love-offerings.

She could feel the mouse's blood seeping through the thin quilt, and she suppressed a groan of revulsion. Orion might interpret any sound she made now as encouragement.

Too late. Orion looked up from where he'd been cleaning blood out of his long fur. He lightly tapped the dead mouse with a paw and it bumped against her bare neck. The tiny corpse had cooled and was tacky with congealing blood. It stuck to her skin.

Penny squealed and her whole body twitched. Castor and Pollux hissed at Orion and bolted from the bed. He hissed in return and Penny felt his claws unsheathe to prick her belly through the blanket. Her arms were free and she twisted to one side to dislodge Orion. He exploded off the bed with an outraged yowl. Penny rolled farther and fell to the floor, dragging the blanket and pillow with her.

The mouse fell on her cheek with a wet squitch and her stomach heaved.

"Get-it-off-get-it-off-get-it-off!" Penny screeched, slapping the mouse away and scrubbing at her skin as she struggled to untangle herself from the blanket. She scooted away from the bed, scanning wildly to see where the mouse had landed.

The room was brighter and she could now see several red splotches on the bed sheet. There was a chunk of pale grey fur stuck to one of the blood stains. She pressed a hand to her stomach to suppress her rising nausea as she spotted the tiny mangled mouse in the corner.

Penny staggered to her feet and nearly screamed again when Orion rubbed his head against her bare calf. His fur was damp. She swatted at him weakly and he raced out of the room and headed for the kitchen, where she could hear Castor meowing piteously for his breakfast.

"You're all going to have to wait until this cat lady's had a hot shower," she shouted, pulling her t-shirt over her head and using it to scrub the ick off her cheek and neck. She jammed her arms into her bathrobe with a shudder and firmly closed the door on the carnage in her bedroom.

Cookbook Hijack

The phone rang and Bobby's head jerked up as he snapped awake. He felt a hot pinch in the back of his neck and glanced guiltily at the dormant computer monitor. He snatched the receiver out of its cradle on the third ring and rubbed his sore neck with his other hand.

"Bobby Fraser," he snapped, trying to sound more awake than he felt.

"Someone to see you," said a bored voice. He could almost hear the receptionist roll her eyes. "Says she's got an appointment."

Click.

Bobby turned his head with the phone still held to his ear. His neck creaked and he winced and swivelled his chair to straighten his body. Judy's desk was near the door, only two cubicles away from Bobby's. She waved a languid arm in his direction and a small woman with bristly white hair grinned at him in recognition.

Mabel Berkeley. Bobby felt his cheeks redden at the memory of his first meeting with Mabel two years ago. She'd just come from a dip in Cricket Lake and he'd been overwhelmed with embarrassment at the sight of the tiny older woman dripping wet in her bra and baggy shorts.

"Nice to see you again, sonny," Mabel said as she dragged over a plastic lawn chair she'd snagged from the waiting area near the door. She set it next to his at the desk and sat with a sigh.

"What can I do for you?" he asked warily.

"You're the one who asked for an interview."

"But that's not for two weeks, and with Dee." He'd recently seen Mabel and Dee on television, being interviewed as part of a special feature about a famous journalist who'd died in Cricket Lake. Bobby had sent Dee Berkeley an email and made an appointment for a phone interview to discuss the impact of the death on their community.

Mabel waved away his protest. "Dee's much too busy with the café to deal with the media. Besides, I'm the official spokesperson for Voodoo Café, and Fiona happened to be coming to Vancouver for the day so I tagged along."

Bobby glanced to his left, where Tom and Lisa were grinning at his discomfiture. They didn't hold interviews in the office, as there were no spare rooms for privacy, only the dubious cover of their four-foot cubicle walls.

Mabel had also noticed their audience. She waved to them, to Bobby's dismay. They trooped over and leaned on the cubicle wall. Bobby tried to convey by eyebrow raising and eye rolling that he wanted them to leave, but they ignored him and focused on Mabel.

"So tell us why you're here," Lisa said.

"Well, Bobby is an old friend and he did such a good job of writing us up last time that we were excited when he called for a follow-up interview."

"Not exactly a follow-up," Bobby said, leaning back in his chair to keep everyone in sight. "I was interested in Tobias Greer, the journalist who wrote his memoirs while he was staying in your town."

"Isn't that the guy who traded himself for a bunch of hostages back in the eighties?" Tom leaned farther over the wall, making the flimsy partition teeter in its frame.

"What was he like?" Lisa asked. "I heard he was pretty hot, for an older guy."

"Hey, who's asking the questions here?" Bobby protested.

Mabel winked at Lisa. "Toby wasn't exactly my type, but he wasn't too bad to look at. He wrote a book all about his life while he stayed with us but it's not in the stores yet." She turned back to Bobby. "So go ahead and ask your questions."

"I just set up the interview yesterday! I haven't even thought about what I want to ask." Bobby wished the others would leave so he could deal with Mabel on his own.

"Bobby is mostly a sports writer," Tom offered helpfully. "He's used to talking to jocks so he'd need time to plan for a more sophisticated interview."

"Hey! That's not fair! No one here does spontaneous interviews. That's how we preserve the professional ideals of the trade." Bobby opened a drawer and took out a spiral notebook. He fished a ballpoint pen out of a mug that was missing its handle. Mabel waited expectantly. He couldn't think of a single question to ask.

Mabel leaned forward and patted Bobby's hand. "That's ok, sonny. I came prepared." She pulled a wrinkled brown envelope from her tote bag and slid the contents onto Bobby's desk.

Lisa leaned over the wall and snatched up the top sheet of paper. "Bacon and Egg Lasagna?" She grabbed another, while avoiding Bobby who was trying to stop her. "Taco Shepherd's Pie? These are recipes."

"They're all award winners," Mabel said proudly, handing Lisa two more pages.

"Wait a minute," Lisa said, laying the sheets side by side on another desk. "There are three different lasagna recipes here."

"This interview isn't about recipes," Bobby protested. "It's about Tobias Greer."

"That's what I'm trying to tell you," Mabel said as she sorted through the stack of papers. "It's about both. Toby said that everyone has a story inside them. He tried to talk me into writing my own memoirs but I don't have the patience for that. Dee suggested I write a recipe book instead." She handed another sheet to Lisa, who wrinkled her nose at the title.

"Strawberry Garlic Jam? Yuck!"

"The first version wasn't too popular," Mabel admitted with a grin. "I'd bought several flats of strawberries and three whole braided ropes of garlic, a couple dozen bulbs or so. I boiled the strawberries and garlic then mashed them up with some sugar." She laughed at the expressions on their faces.

"It took me nearly a year to finish off the two dozen jars by myself. Most people wouldn't even taste it. Then someone suggested I roast the garlic first and add it to the cooked strawberries with some balsamic vinegar. Kinda fancy but tasted good enough to win this year's competition."

"I can't write a story about a cookbook," Bobby said and rolled his chair away from the desk.

"The paper's looking for more submissions for the new food supplement," Tom offered. "You could easily get that gig."

"I'm not a food writer," Bobby protested. "I write serious, informative essays."

Tom rolled his eyes. "Your last three interviews were with hockey players."

"Hockey is an important part of our Canadian heritage."

"Sure, everyone was dying to read your exclusive series on the Canucks' favourite video games." Tom ducked to avoid the pen Bobby threw at him.

"Boys, that's enough," Lisa said. She handed a page to Tom. "You'd like the Taco Shepherd's Pie. It's got lots of peppers and hot sauce in the meat and crumbled corn chips on top."

She turned back to Mabel. "Tell us more about your cookbook."

"Well," Mabel began, "I don't really have enough for a whole book. That's why I was glad that Bobby contacted us."

"I contacted Dee," Bobby muttered.

"Shh," Mabel and Lisa said together.

"Okay, so here's my idea," Mabel continued. "I thought you could write a series about our annual cooking contest, starting with lasagna."

"You want me to write a story about lasagna?"

"Not just any lasagna," Lisa said gleefully. "Bacon and Egg Lasagna!"

"I could help you write them, if that's the problem," Mabel said.

Tom snickered. "Come on, Bobby. You know you love lasagna."

"And bacon," Lisa added. "Look, they're all pretty easy to make from what I can tell." She thrust a page under Bobby's nose. "This one is layered with bacon omelettes instead of noodles. Oh god, that sounds delicious!"

"That's the fancy one that Fiona came up with. She made it up for those who don't want to use noodles. Mine is the one with hard-boiled eggs cut in half. You set them all side by side – flat part down – on the bottom of the pan and then add enough sauce to cover them. Then you put all your usual layers of noodles and cheese over that. The top layer is bacon, all woven together like a mat."

"You're making me drool. What about the third one?" Tom asked.

"That's Dee's low-calorie version. She scrambled the eggs until they were dry and fried the bacon to a crisp for crumbling. Then she just mixed it all into the tomato sauce and made regular lasagna with it. It's a little boring but cute with the two sunny-side-ups on the top for eyes and a strip of bacon for a smile."

"None of this has anything to do with Tobias Greer," Bobby complained. He stood up but Mabel's chair blocked the only exit from the tiny cubicle, trapping him where he stood. He dropped back into his chair with a sigh.

"So make the first installment about how Toby inspired me to share my creations and then just launch into the food." Mabel patted his knee and he banged his chair into the wall, making the partition teeter.

"If it's too much for you then I'll write it," Lisa offered. "I think it's a fantastic idea, but you're right about the style. You're more of a jock writer and might not have the right flair to pull this off."

Bobby glanced at Lisa suspiciously. She'd won two awards for her features on local artists and he'd studied every word, trying to figure out what made them so appealing. He opened his mouth with no idea of what he was going to say but Mabel beat him to it.

"Thanks for the offer, Lisa, but I want Bobby for this job."

"Could I copy some of these to try at home?"

"Sure, as long as you don't share any of the recipes until Bobby's published them." Mabel and Lisa gathered up all the loose pages and headed for the copy room, chatting about ingredients.

"So are you going to take on the assignment?" Tom asked as he picked up a stray page off the floor and set it on the desk.

"I don't think I have a choice." Bobby glanced at the page Tom had rescued, and groaned. "French Onion Soup Jello. This just keeps getting worse."

"Naw, it'll be great," Tom said and slapped Bobby on the back with a laugh. "Everybody loves jello."

About the Author

Monique Jacob has been writing stories and songs since her first tortured-teen ramblings and she's never managed to outgrow the habit. She stares at the walls an awful lot and has yet to convince anyone that this is when she's working the hardest.

Born in Germany, Monique has moved 29 times in 9 cities and now makes her home on the West Coast, somewhere between Seattle and Vancouver – as the crow flies.

Voodoo Mystery Tour is her second novel and the sequel to *Tye Dye Voodoo*. Follow Monique on Facebook and at moniquejacob.ca

(Photo by Geotectomy Photography)